Praise For
Bob Balaban's
McGROWL #1:
BEWARE OF DOG

"Balaban unleashes hilarious McGrowl! . . . Filled with absurd humor and fun, cartoonlike action."
— *USA Today*

"Mr. Balaban takes his obvious love of language and wordplay and creates a magical tale of a mind-reading dog that all young minds should read. An intelligent and plentiful debut."
— *Jamie Lee Curtis*

"For anybody who has ever had a dog, loved a dog, or wanted a dog. A great adventure beautifully written. I hope Bob writes the next one about me."
— *Richard Dreyfuss*

(#2)

IT'S A DOG'S LIFE

#2

IT'S A DOG'S LIFE

Bob Balaban

A Storyopolis Book

AN
APPLE
PAPERBACK

SCHOLASTIC INC.
New York Toronto London Auckland Sydney
Mexico City New Delhi Hong Kong Buenos Aires

ISBN 0-439-43455-6

12 11 10 9 8 7 6 5   4 5 6 7 8/0
                                              40
Printed in the U.S.A.
First Scholastic printing, March 2003

For Joe and Emma and Wilson,
who love golden retrievers
as much as I do
— B. B.

Contents

CHAPTER ONE
Finders Keepers

Thomas was getting worried. It was five-thirty, and McGrowl was nowhere to be seen. Suppertime was the one time of day the dog could be counted on to be on time. Thomas sauntered into the kitchen and did his best to appear casual. "Any golden retrievers in this part of the house?"

"Better not be," his mother swiftly replied, furiously whisking a mass of gooey egg whites into foamy little peaks. "Your father will be home any minute."

Mr. Wiggins was doing his best to get used

to the idea of living under the same roof as a dog, but he was still frightened out of his wits at the very sight of McGrowl. In fact, he had made Thomas take a solemn oath never to allow the animal anywhere near him.

Every night Mr. Wiggins listened to another one of the desensitizing tapes Mrs. Wiggins had ordered for him. The series was titled "Pets, Panic, and You," and it wasn't helping. Last night's tape gently urged Mr. Wiggins to put his fear into a paper bag, crumple it up, and throw it into the garbage. The voice on the tape droned on: "Tell yourself the animal is your friend and you have nothing to fear."

"Fat chance," Thomas's father had said to himself as he checked the lock on his door and clutched the can of Dog-gone he had taken to carrying with him everywhere. The tapes were supposed to be making Mr. Wiggins less afraid of dogs but seemed to be having the opposite effect.

"I'll be in the backyard," Thomas suddenly announced, and ran outside to look for McGrowl.

"That's nice," Mrs. Wiggins replied. She wasn't really paying attention. "Whatever you do, don't get that shirt rumpled. I don't have time to iron it again."

She had a million things to do before Mr. Lundquist and his wife arrived for dinner. Mr. Lundquist was Thomas's father's boss, and whenever he came to dinner, which was about once in a blue moon, everybody had to look their very best.

Thomas could tell in a flash that McGrowl was definitely not in the backyard.

It seemed like only yesterday that McGrowl had come to live with Thomas. Actually it had been three weeks, two days, and sixteen hours. Thomas had come upon the bedraggled animal in the ravine one rainy Saturday afternoon, and it had been love at first bark.

The boy still couldn't believe his good fortune. He had been asking for a dog ever since he was old enough to talk. And although nobody but his friend Violet knew it, this was no ordinary pet.

McGrowl's molecules had undergone a massive transformation after an unfortunate encounter with a power plant and about thirty million volts of electricity. A perfectly ordinary dog chased a pesky cat into an energy field and emerged with bionic superpowers the likes of which had never been seen in any animal. Or person, for that matter.

The dog was the strongest, fastest, and smartest animal in the world. But even more amazingly, McGrowl shared with Thomas a telepathic connection that would have made him the envy of every boy in his school had Thomas chosen to reveal it. But Thomas and Violet decided long ago never to reveal the dog's superpowers to anyone.

IT'S A DOG'S LIFE

Like Batman and Superman before him, McGrowl would keep his extraordinary abilities under wraps. Only the forces of evil he combated so courageously would ever come to know the special powers he possessed.

Thomas finished searching under the crawl space beneath the garage and forlornly surveyed the empty yard.

The boy was frantic. The dog wasn't on the roof, or up a tree, or in any of his other favorite hiding places. Thomas dashed across the street and went straight to Violet's house. She would know what to do. A minute later Thomas and his best and only friend were combing the neighborhood.

"Has he ever done this before?" Violet inquired.

Thomas thought for a moment. "Not really."

Violet did her best to put a positive spin on things. "Well, let's not jump to any hasty conclusions."

"Right," Thomas replied tersely, and redoubled his efforts. But the leap had already been taken, and both children were absolutely certain that the dog was in some kind of danger. "Here, McGrowl," he yelled.

There was a force of evil on the loose somewhere in Cedar Springs. A malevolent stranger and his wicked accomplice had attempted to kidnap McGrowl several weeks ago and then had vanished into thin air. What if they were back? What if they had already captured McGrowl?

In their quest to destroy the peaceful little town of Cedar Springs, the stranger and his accomplice could take on the shape and form of anyone they chose. They would be impossible to recognize the next time they struck.

In fact, at that very moment the evil duo was hatching a scheme so clever, so diabolical, it would require every ounce of Thomas's and Violet's — and especially McGrowl's — ingenuity and abilities to undo it.

And then they spotted McGrowl. He was five yards down the street and across the alley, waiting for the neighborhood cat to emerge for her evening constitutional. He hated that cat. He was sitting still as a statue as he prepared to pounce on his prey. He looked so happy and excited Thomas couldn't even get angry. "I should have known," he said quietly and with much relief.

"So where's the darned cat?" Violet whispered.

Thomas pointed overhead. The cat, sensing the presence of the dog, was carefully and silently creeping out an upstairs window and slinking onto a large branch of the tree that had grown up alongside the house. McGrowl's superhearing detected the bending of a twig immediately. He looked up, saw the cat, and realized he'd been outsmarted. By a lowly feline. This was almost more than a grown dog could bear.

"You'd better get back in your room before my dad gets home. We've got company coming." Thomas turned on his heel and started back to the house.

McGrowl decided to obey. He was eager to leave the scene of his failure. Silently, he cursed the cat and immediately started hatching another plan to capture her.

"Don't even think about it," the boy replied firmly, and kept on walking. The telepathic connection worked in both directions. The dog gave him an extremely sheepish and apologetic look and followed obediently. "Good dog," Thomas said, reaching down to scratch him behind the ears, his favorite scratching place. McGrowl could be very well behaved when he felt like it. Trouble was, he didn't always feel like it.

CHAPTER TWO
Guess Who's Coming to Dinner?

At last they were home. The smells of Mrs. Wiggins's famous chicken potpie wafted through the house, causing McGrowl's nose to twitch and his eyes to water.

"If you're really good I'll save you a piece." McGrowl shot Thomas a testy look. "Okay, two pieces." The dog didn't seem convinced. "And cherry pie with vanilla ice cream." The dog eagerly licked his lips and bounded up the stairs.

Violet hurried off to her house, and Thomas

ran upstairs to change for dinner. As he searched for just the right pair of pants, his thoughts turned to the Big Dog Show. Obedience trials were tomorrow after school. Thomas had been dreaming about having a pet to enroll at the annual event for as long as he could remember and was eager to show off McGrowl's prowess. The top five dogs in the obedience trials would go on to compete in the Big Dog Show, which was in several weeks.

Lewis Musser, the class bully, was already telling everybody his dog, Spike, would be taking home the grand prize — an enormous silver trophy. But Thomas was planning on giving him a run for his money.

The fact that McGrowl was able to effortlessly understand everything Thomas was thinking was definitely going to be a plus in the command and obey division. Whether he would *feel* like obeying was a different story.

Thomas finished combing his hair and ran downstairs.

Mr. Wiggins was in the living room with his boss, Al Lundquist, attempting to impress him. Mrs. Lundquist was in the powder room freshening up. Thomas was never exactly sure what that term meant. Nothing he ever did in the bathroom seemed to make anything any fresher.

Thomas's brother, Roger, loved chicken potpie, but he was having a study date with Violet's sister, Alicia. If he continued getting D's in chemistry he wouldn't be able to play in the all-city playoffs. So far the only thing that studying with Alicia seemed to be improving was Roger's wardrobe. Every time he went over to her house he put on a new outfit and a ton of the cologne his father brought back from the "perfume makers of America" convention.

"You look very nice, honey," said Mrs. Wiggins to her son. "But your shirt's sticking out a little in the back." Thomas stuck the offending piece of material quickly back into his pants and looked around the gleaming kitchen. His mother had somehow managed to cook an elaborate five-course meal without dirtying a single dish. The room looked as immaculate as it did this morning before breakfast.

"This is a very big night for your father," she said, arranging mint sprigs artfully on a beautiful lacquered tray filled with a dizzying array of condiments. "He's about this far away from landing a wonderful new account." She demonstrated by holding up two of the sprigs a fraction of an inch apart from each other. "We want to make sure everything goes perfectly."

She whirled out the door, placed the tray carefully on the dining room table, and tinkled a little crystal bell that was reserved for only the most special of occasions. "Dinner, everyone," she called out in a voice as delicate as the bell.

The candles twinkled gaily as Thomas's father unfolded his ingenious campaign for Mr. Lundquist's most important new client, Mel Muchnick. Mr. Muchnick was running for mayor, and the public relations firm of Lundquist & Beane had been selected to design and execute a strategy for the entire campaign, including a television commercial.

Mr. Wiggins was desperate to be chosen to oversee this monumental task. Thomas had to admit everything certainly was going well. Mr. Lundquist seemed especially interested in the citywide parade and handshaking tour Mr. Wiggins was proposing with a kind of precision even Thomas found impressive.

Mr. Lundquist leaned forward, deposited his many chins on his folded hands, and listened with an intensity that could only be described as ferocious. Mr. Wiggins finished his proposal and paused dramatically. Beads of sweat glistened on his forehead. Every eye at the table turned to Mr. Lundquist to see which way the tide was turning.

"What I want to know is this," he finally announced, polishing off his third helping of potatoes Lyonnaise. "Why aren't I paying you more?" Everyone laughed merrily, and Mr. Wiggins aimed a secret little smile in Mrs. Wiggins's direction. She beamed back excitedly.

And then Thomas noticed movement on the stairs. His heart practically stopped. The tip of a long, bushy yellow tail could be seen speeding past the little hallway that separated the kitchen from the dining room. "Oh, no," he groaned softly.

"Something the matter, sweetheart?" Mrs. Wiggins asked casually. The answer was a resounding yes, but Thomas just stared into space and tried to think of a way to get the dog back upstairs without anyone noticing. Evidently, the smell of all that delicious food had inflamed the dog's insatiable appetite, and he had snuck down for a predinner snack. "Honey, are you all right?" Mrs. Wiggins was getting concerned.

"Need water." Thomas could scarcely get the words out. He lurched from the table and started for the kitchen.

"You sit right back down, son. I'll bring in the pitcher," said Thomas's father. "I think we all could use a little ice-cold *agua*." Everyone chuckled appreciatively as Mr. Wiggins, feeling just a little bit full of himself, strode proudly into the kitchen. Thomas sat back down and waited for disaster to strike. It didn't take long.

Mr. Wiggins entered the kitchen and immediately spotted McGrowl standing right smack in the middle of the kitchen table. He froze, terrified. The dog was finishing the last scrap of the pie. His face was covered with ice cream. Juice from the cherries was dribbling down his chin and all over his paws. If you didn't know better, you might think the dog was foaming at the mouth and covered in blood, which was, of course, precisely what Mr. Wiggins thought.

"There's nothing to fear . . . nothing at all . . . no fear . . . no fear," he mumbled incoherently to himself, and started tiptoeing backward, hoping the dog wouldn't notice him. Unfortunately, he knocked over a chair and crashed into the wall, frightening McGrowl, who looked up abruptly and slipped on some cherry juice. The dog went flying across the room, right into the arms of the petrified man. All Mr. Wiggins could do was cry for help.

"Monster — monster — there's a monster in the kitchen." McGrowl flew out the window faster than the proverbial speeding bullet. The entire table scrambled in to see what was the matter. A red-faced Mr. Wiggins sat on the floor, covered with ice cream and cherries, crying. Nobody could think of a thing to say.

At last Mrs. Lundquist broke the ice. "I guess he was just too hungry to wait for the rest of us." Mr. Lundquist thought this was just about the funniest thing he had ever heard and began laughing uproariously. Mrs. Lundquist joined in happily, followed by a somewhat tentative Mrs. Wiggins and a decidedly shaky Thomas.

Even Mr. Wiggins managed to croak out a couple of hearty guffaws. But he most certainly did not enjoy playing the fool on his big night. He promised himself then and there to make sure this sort of thing never, ever happened again.

McGrowl was in big trouble.

CHAPTER THREE
Crime and Punishment

McGrowl slept well. Thomas didn't. He tossed and turned and worried the night away. He had bad news for his new friend. McGrowl would not be going to school with Thomas in the morning. He wouldn't be competing in the dog show, either. On those two points Mr. Wiggins was adamant.

"You're lucky I'm not sending that animal back where it came from," Mr. Wiggins sternly admonished Thomas. Of course, this was clearly an idle threat. Neither Thomas nor his father had the remotest idea where that was.

McGrowl rolled over peacefully in Thomas's warm, cozy bed, blissfully unaware of the consequences of his actions the night before. He was dreaming of mashed potatoes. A dollop of golden yellow butter was melting right in the middle of the mound. Rich brown gravy floated all around the edges of the platter.

The dog started gobbling enormous bites of the stuff. Unfortunately, what he was actually eating was Thomas's pillow. His sharp incisors tore large holes in the ticking, and feathers were flying everywhere.

Thomas was already up and had just run in to look for his windbreaker. "What are you doing!" he exclaimed, seeing the mess.

McGrowl woke up, spit out a mouthful of feathers, and wondered the exact same thing when he saw that Thomas was dressed and attempting to leave without him. Who knew what evil was lurking just around the corner? He was not about to let his boy go to school unchaperoned.

Besides, he loved getting his daily treat from the jolly crossing guard and took great pride in the fact that Thomas always let him carry his books. He never dropped a single one and always double-checked to make certain Thomas hadn't left an important homework assignment behind.

And anyway, he was looking forward to the Big Dog Show tryouts this afternoon. Only the first five to place in the obedience trials would be allowed to compete in next month's finals. The winner of the finals would take home the gleaming silver trophy. He felt a warm glow all over when he thought about how proud Thomas was going to be when they carried it home and put it on the mantel. He was going to school today, that's all there was to it.

IT'S A DOG'S LIFE

The dog gave Thomas a look that managed to convey both enormous sadness and great annoyance simultaneously. The expression had the desired effect. Thomas was instantly engulfed in a wave of guilt.

"It's not my fault," Thomas began. "You can't go to school with me today. Dad says so." As the boy did his best to make order of the extremely rumpled bed, McGrowl lowered his head and looked as if he might begin to cry. "Please don't do that. I feel bad enough as it is."

Thomas located the jacket and started out of the room. McGrowl ran to the door and threw himself between it and the boy. "I'll come home right after school. I promise." The dog didn't budge. "We're gonna get in serious trouble if you don't do exactly what my father says." Still no response. "He might not even let you stay here anymore, McGrowl."

The dog reluctantly moved away from the

door. "Good boy," Thomas said, and leaned over to give him a hug. "You really wanted to be in the dog show, didn't you?" The dog let out a pitiful moan. "There's always next year. We'll have lots more time to practice." The dog pointed his big brown nose straight up at the ceiling and howled pathetically. "No more complaining. It's just the way it is."

The boy was out the door and halfway down the stairs. McGrowl let out a few more howls. When he saw they weren't doing any good, he gave up, looked out the window, and sulked. At last he spied Mr. Wiggins hurrying into the garage and then out again in his shiny new Oldsmobile. Mrs. Wiggins ran out to borrow a pinch of saffron from Alicia's mom.

The dog sprang into action. He pushed open the window with his sturdy snout and leaped onto the roof. He watched as a Federal Express truck headed past and quickly jumped right onto it. He would be at Thomas's school in a couple of minutes.

The bell for first period rang, and Thomas took his seat for homeroom. He had just finished the unhappy task of explaining to the lower school principal that his dog wasn't feeling well and wouldn't be able to be in the dog show today.

McGrowl waited patiently outside the window, careful not to let Thomas see him. He surveyed the area around the little school. He was always on the lookout for the evil duo who had abducted him and almost kidnapped the boy earlier that month. Thankfully, they were nowhere to be seen. Suddenly, McGrowl heard his name being called.

"McGrowl! McGrowl!"

But where was the voice coming from? Surely no one in the building had spotted him. The bush he was hiding beside rendered him practically invisible. Again he heard the insistent call. The dog looked this way and that. And then he focused his powerful sense of hearing in the direction of the Wiggins's house.

As clearly as if she were standing right next to him, he could hear Mrs. Wiggins's voice calling him. And then, even though school was a good three miles away from home, he concentrated with all his might, and Thomas's bedroom window came into perfect view. He could see Mrs. Wiggins sticking her neck out and yelling down the street.

"You come back here this instant. I mean it, McGrowl. Are you listening to me? You're a naughty, naughty dog."

And before you could say Jiminy Cricket, the dog was off in a flash. He went into hypergear and sped back home so fast he was almost invisible. If you had decided to look in his direction, all you would have seen was a bunch of leaves swirling around what looked like a yellow tornado. The entire journey took less than three seconds. Before she even had a chance to turn around, the dog made a beeline into the house, up the stairs, and into the bed.

As Mrs. Wiggins headed toward the door, McGrowl jumped out of the bed, wagging his tail as if he had been there the whole time. He rushed over to Mrs. Wiggins, licked her hand happily, and barked a cheery hello. The poor woman nearly jumped out of her skin.

"Where — what — how in the world?" She couldn't manage to get anything else out. She rubbed her eyes to see if she was dreaming. She had searched high and low and found not a single trace of dog anywhere. "Strange. Very strange."

McGrowl leaped out of the window for the second time that morning and hurried back to school and his special hiding place in the bushes by the windows. Meanwhile, Thomas and the rest of his class were in the process of receiving some pretty disturbing news.

CHAPTER FOUR
Something Strange

"Someone has stolen the class treasury," Miss Thompson announced ruefully.

You could have heard a pin drop. She continued. "That someone had better come forward immediately and put the money back in my desk, where they found it. Let us put our heads down on our desks and hum loudly."

Everyone, including Miss Thompson, put their heads down and started humming. This was the signal for the thief to return the stolen property and then hurry back to his or her desk. At last Miss Thompson looked up and called for the class to stop humming. She felt in the drawer and was clearly disappointed and somewhat surprised. The missing thirty-four dollars and twenty-five cents was nowhere to be seen.

Thomas and Violet exchanged quizzical glances. What was going on? Thomas had heard on the news last night about a robbery over at the hardware store. Violet reminded him that her cousin's tricycle had been stolen only yesterday. Was this part of a larger pattern?

In all of his years at Stevenson, no one had ever stolen so much as a piece of chalk. Lewis Musser took a lot of things, but not without asking first. You never dared say no when Lewis asked. But that wasn't the same as stealing.

Thomas wondered for a moment if perhaps the evil duo had returned and was up to one of their devilish schemes. The thought quickly vanished when he saw the unmistakable tip of a yellow tail wagging happily outside the window. Thomas quietly sidled over to the back of the room. "What are you doing here?" he asked softly. McGrowl pretended he was hard of hearing and burrowed deeper into the bushes. "Go home, go home. Please, whatever you do, go home."

"I beg your pardon, young man?" Miss Thompson didn't seem amused. "Why should I go home?"

The class started to laugh hysterically. Miss Thompson took up the large ruler she kept by the side of her desk and smashed it loudly against the blackboard, her swift and efficient way of demanding silence. She got it. Her gleaming eyes seemed to bore a hole into the boy while she waited for a reply.

"I repeat," she intoned dryly, "why should I go home?" Again there was silence. "Cat got your tongue?" McGrowl heard the word *cat* and tensed up even more.

Thomas was so terrified all he could muster was a barely audible "uh-uh."

"Uh-uh, what?" came the angry reply.

"Uh-uh, Miss Thompson?" Evidently that was the response she was looking for.

"You will clean the erasers for the next three days. During recess you will arrange the chairs for chorus. After lunch on Tuesday . . ." As she droned on with her list of annoying punishments, Thomas's attention drifted over to the sound of distant trumpets, and then the sound of drums beating rhythmically, and the tinkling of a dozen glockenspiels. Something very much like a parade seemed to be making its way toward the school. Everyone leaped out of their chairs and rushed to the windows to get a better look.

Miss Thompson picked up her ruler again

and rapped it furiously against her desk so many times that it broke in half. "Order in the class, order in the class," she hollered as she waved pieces of the broken ruler wildly about in each hand. No one paid the slightest attention to her.

The brass section started playing "Hail to the Chief," while a corps of majorettes in red-and-gold uniforms tossed flyers bearing the picture of a heavyset, smiling fellow into the gathering crowd. By now the procession was only a couple of hundred feet away from Stevenson.

McGrowl forgot he was supposed to be hiding. He rushed over to the throng and ran around, barking and wagging his tail furiously. He loved a good parade as much as any red-blooded American dog. By now the entire middle school had come out to see what was happening. Even Miss Thompson peeked out of the window discreetly to watch the proceedings. Thomas and Violet edged forward to get a better look.

A smiling man riding on a beautifully decorated float stepped forward. He looked exactly like the man on the flyers, only he was a little shorter and a little heavier.

The car pulling the float came to a halt so suddenly he almost fell over, and everyone gasped. He teetered precariously for a moment and finally caught his balance. At last he spoke. A hush fell quickly over the milling throng.

The man yelled into a bullhorn. "I'm Mel Muchnick. I'm running for mayor of this glorious town, and I'm so happy I could scream." His booming voice reverberated loudly throughout the area. McGrowl covered his ears with his paws. The man *was* screaming.

And pretty soon the crowd was screaming, too. Thomas's father was right. A rousing parade certainly was proving to be a brilliant way to kick off a mayoral campaign. Every time the man spoke he was cheered and applauded. He promised lower taxes and higher buildings. He was for grandmothers and babies and against crime and pollution. The crowd was in an absolute frenzy.

Thomas and Violet helped pass out scarves and hats. A VOTE FOR MEL MUCHNICK IS A HAPPY VOTE was emblazoned on each and every one of them.

McGrowl took his paws down from his ears and listened closely. He couldn't understand everything the man was saying, but his loud and friendly voice certainly was reassuring. The dog didn't put up the slightest fuss when someone leaned over and put a hat and a scarf on him.

And then Mel Muchnick raised his hands for silence. Even the birds stopped chirping. He made a long, dramatic pause. For a second, Thomas thought that he had forgotten his lines. At last he spoke, quietly but with great feeling.

"I love this country. I love this town. I love this neighborhood. And I love each and every one of you." The crowd went absolutely mad. Muchnick shook hands and kissed babies and smiled joyously. Photographers aimed their cameras and snapped away.

And then Thomas noticed his father anxiously observing the proceedings from the rear of the car that was pulling the float. He had written the candidate's speech himself, with only a teeny bit of help from Mrs. Wiggins. Every last detail of the parade, however, was his, down to the tassels on the majorettes' high white boots. And he was very proud.

Thomas rushed over to McGrowl to warn him to hide. Before he could get there, someone scooped up the dog and placed him on the platform next to the candidate. Short of a miracle there was absolutely no chance his father wouldn't notice. "This is it," Thomas said to himself. "This is really it."

McGrowl, still wearing his hat and scarf, posed adorably for the photographers as if he knew exactly what was going on, which, of course, he did. He loved the attention. He held perfectly still while Muchnick patted him on the head. He even held up his paw to shake hands with the mayor-to-be while a thousand flashbulbs snapped and crackled.

Thomas couldn't help but notice the look that came over his father's face when he spotted the furry source of the photographers' attention. "Come on down, Henry Wiggins!" Muchnick bellowed. The rest of the blood drained quickly from Mr. Wiggins's already pale face.

McGrowl was off the leash, so a terrified Mr. Wiggins waved from the safety of the rear of the car and mouthed several nervous noes. Muchnick, however, realizing this was a perfect opportunity for a group shot, wasn't about to take no for an answer.

And then, much to Mr. Wiggins's chagrin, Mel Muchnick started a rousing chorus of "We want Wiggins," and three hundred cheering onlookers eagerly joined in the chant. "Wiggins, Wiggins," they screamed as they threw their hats in the air and waved their arms wildly.

Mr. Wiggins protested violently as a couple of eager campaign workers pried him loose from the back of the car and started pushing him forward and onto the platform.

Thomas and Violet held their breath as they watched poor Mr. Wiggins being maneuvered closer and closer to the object of his greatest terror. "What if he faints in front of all these people?" Violet asked. "Think Muchnick'll have him fired?"

"In a heartbeat," Thomas replied without even thinking.

But wonder of wonders, Mr. Wiggins didn't faint. He summoned every ounce of courage he could and remained upright. Shaky, but upright. The crowd grew still as photographers drew in closer for the all-important group photo. McGrowl looked discreetly away from Mr. Wiggins, not even daring to catch his eye, as the candidate stationed himself right in between the two of them, much to Mr. Wiggins's relief.

"Shake hands," Muchnick whispered urgently under his breath. Mr. Wiggins held out a hand and attempted to shake Muchnick's. "No, you idiot, shake the dog's hand."

"Oh," Mr. Wiggins glumly replied. "You want me to shake the dog's hand?" But he didn't make a move.

"Well, what are you waiting for?" Muchnick was clearly getting annoyed. Again the crowd chanted, "Shake his hand, shake his hand."

McGrowl held out a paw and attempted to smile sweetly at Mr. Wiggins, which was something of a mistake. Instead of appearing to smile, the dog's rather large and unwieldy lips took on the ominous appearance of a snarl. "Could you please restrain the animal?" was all Mr. Wiggins could manage to say.

"Don't be ridiculous," Muchnick replied. "Let's get on with it."

So Mr. Wiggins held his breath, leaned down, and put out his quavering hand. It was the closest he had ever been to a dog, and certainly the first time he had voluntarily attempted to touch one. McGrowl did his best to hold absolutely rock-solid still. He wished he had remembered to ask Thomas to clip his nails. They were somewhat longer than he felt Mr. Wiggins would like.

Three hundred people cheered as a host of photographers busily snapped away. Mr.

Wiggins looked toward heaven, said a quiet prayer, made contact with a dog, and lived to tell the tale.

Thomas could hardly believe his eyes. He tugged excitedly at Violet's sweater.

"I see, I see," she replied softly. "Who would have thunk it?"

And then, not to be outdone by his campaign manager, Mr. Muchnick got down on his hands and knees and crawled over and kissed the dog smack on the lips. McGrowl wasn't used to anyone taking such liberties with him, let alone strangers who were running for mayor. He quickly pulled back and wiped his mouth discreetly with his paw.

He noticed how bristly the man's mustache was. He noticed that the man appeared to be wearing a great deal of makeup. And then he noticed a strange but familiar odor. It was difficult to detect at first because the man had gone to some length to cover it up with a heavy dose of a musky, bitter cologne. McGrowl recognized the smell but couldn't put his paw on precisely where he had noticed it before.

After another sustained round of cheers and testimonials, Mr. Wiggins located Thomas and begrudgingly gave McGrowl one last chance. He would be allowed to compete in the dog show trials after all.

"But," Mr. Wiggins firmly reminded Thomas, "any more bad behavior and we're talking obedience school. We're talking no dessert ever. We're talking dry dog food and water."

And then Muchnick and his noisy caravan headed off to the mall on the far side of town for another rally. The crowd of happy students and teachers waved good-bye at last, put aside their new hats and scarves, and headed back to their classrooms. They were in for a big surprise.

CHAPTER FIVE
Best in Show

The bell for last period rang, and students started swarming up and down the staircase like an army of eager ants. Tryouts for the Big Dog Show were about to begin, and no one wanted to miss a single moment.

As they rushed and pushed and pulled their way to the field, where the exciting event was about to take place, everyone was buzzing about the mysterious incident that had just occurred.

Sometime during Mel Muchnick's speech, while the entire population of Stevenson upper and lower was outside watching the festivities, a mysterious stranger had been busy rifling through Mabel Rabkin's office.

Miss Rabkin, the beloved school registrar, eighty years old if she was a day, had returned to find hundreds of manila folders spread randomly around her office. Every student who had ever attended Stevenson, even for a semester, had a permanent file in this hallowed room. The files contained records of absolutely everything pertaining to each student.

Miss Rabkin was unable to tell immediately if anything had been stolen. She couldn't imagine what use the folders would be to anyone. The purpose of the break-in remained a mystery. And all the more unsettling because of it.

Officer Nelson was on the scene in a flash and dusting for fingerprints. He had only just completed his mail-order course in this tricky field and was having a fair amount of trouble locating a single print. He was highly allergic to the dust with which he had to cover the fingerprints and kept sneezing and obliterating the clues.

As Thomas hurried past the little room, he made a mental note to make sure to return after Officer Nelson was finished. He was prepared to do a little sleuthing of his own.

"Where's McGrowl? Prelims are about to start," said Violet as she caught up with Thomas. "Points off for lateness, you know." The two friends hurried out the door and started for the soccer field. As if on cue, the big yellow dog came bounding over.

"Good boy," Thomas said, giving the fur on the top of McGrowl's head an affectionate pat. "Ready for the trials?"

The dog wagged his tail eagerly and sent Thomas a telepathic message indicating resounding confidence. At that moment Lewis

Musser and Spike attempted to push rudely ahead of Thomas and McGrowl. McGrowl discreetly stuck out a paw in their path, and both dog and boy tumbled instantly to the ground. Lewis wasn't the least bit injured, but his feelings were. McGrowl just looked in the other direction and pretended to be interested in a passing butterfly.

"I saw that, Wiggins. Apologize or you're dead meat." Lewis was nothing if not direct.

"I didn't do anything," Thomas replied hastily.

"He didn't. Pinkies to the sky." Violet kissed her two little fingers and pointed them straight up. "I swear on the life of my parakeet."

"Yeah? Well, just in case, I'm putting both of you on my list, and you know what that means." And then Lewis and his equally arrogant dog hurried off to torture someone else.

Unfortunately, both Thomas and Violet

knew *exactly* what that meant. Once Lewis put you on his list you had to be especially nice to him and get off the list quickly, or he would turn your life into a nightmare.

McGrowl sent Thomas a short but heartfelt apology. He hadn't meant to get him in trouble. "I accept," Thomas answered gratefully.

"It's rude to communicate telepathically when there are others present." Violet tried not to sound jealous, but she was. Thomas alone held the thrilling connection to McGrowl's mind.

The soccer field was filled with yelling children and barking dogs. Little Esther Mueller, a second-grader with high hopes of winning at least a letter of commendation, tried to calm her Chihuahua, Rumpelstiltskin. The high-strung little pet was refusing to wear the mini matador jacket and sombrero she had made for him from a single piece of blue felt.

The dog shook his head violently, dislodging

his enormous hat. He jumped up and down, frantically chewing away at the beaded matador jacket that hung in tatters around his quivering torso. Little Esther snapped her fingers loudly and yelled the command that had worked perfectly well the day before: "Cease and obey, cease and obey." She was practically in tears, but the dog was beyond reasoning.

"Placesss, please." Principal Grimble loved the way his voice sounded on the microphone and took great care to enunciate every one of his consonants crisply and clearly. He had no idea how ridiculous it made him sound. "Will the ownersss and their petssss assemble immediately on the farrrr side of the fieldddd."

The announcement caused a desperate flurry of activity among children and dogs. For many of the participants, simply getting their animals to cooperate long enough to get into a line was utterly hopeless.

McGrowl trotted obediently and quickly to his place on the starting line and carefully eyed the competition. Dogs of all shapes and sizes got into position.

Stuart Seltzer's sturdy little beagle, Franklin, looked promising but held no real threat. Sophie Morris's poodle, Fluffy, simply looked foolish. McGrowl was not about to lose any sleep over a dog that allowed her fur to be cut so that her legs looked like lollipops.

Principal Grimble blew his whistle and called for silence. And he got it. *Let the games begin,* McGrowl thought to himself. Thomas had to admit that he, too, was raring to go.

CHAPTER SIX
Survival of the Fittest

"Will Fluffy and SSSophie Morrisss please come forwarddd," Principal Grimble enunciated boldly from his viewing stand near the finish line. Principal Grimble pulled out his reading glasses and referred to a bunch of three-by-five note cards he kept in his bulging pockets. He continued.

"Fluffy is a two-year-olddd poodle that loves childrennn and other dogsss and enjoys playing with chew stickkkks and pull toysss." He looked up. "And who doesn't?" He chuck-

led at his little joke, but nobody else seemed
to think it was very funny.

McGrowl watched as dog and master
moved to the front of a large obstacle course.
He carefully surveyed the randomly placed
cans, bottles, and wastebaskets that littered
the field. Each team had to weave around the
objects as quickly as they could. Points were
taken off if they knocked over anything.
McGrowl knew the course backward and
forward (he had come yesterday — and pre-
viewed it) and could have completed it blind-
folded if necessary.

The very first step was to remove the leash
from the dog. This, for many, was the hardest
part of the entire event. Who knew whether
the pet might suddenly decide to make a
break for home or escape to the nearest fire
hydrant?

The crowd watched nervously as Sophie
reached down, removed the leash, and

slipped her poodle a piece of gingersnap she had been saving since recess. Fluffy eagerly took the bribe and moved forward through the course, following closely and obediently at her master's side. So far, so good.

Even Thomas had to admit she was doing surprisingly well. As they came into the homestretch, dog and master had managed to avoid knocking over a single object. The boy looked over at McGrowl anxiously. The dog didn't respond. He was busily observing wind conditions. Overqualified though he was for the task at hand, McGrowl was taking nothing for granted.

Sophie Morris's friends and family quietly hoisted a large banner that read WE LOVE YOU, FLUFFY. Dog and master twisted their way in and around the complicated pathways.

And then the poor dog made a tragic mistake. Thinking she had reached the end of the course, she jumped up, suddenly and unexpectedly, onto Sophie. The girl was taken off balance and fell backward, knocking over three or four of the obstacles.

A gasp arose from the crowd. Sophie looked over expectantly at Mr. Grimble, as if he might offer a reprieve. He didn't. Distracted and disillusioned, Sophie continued and managed to knock over every single object that remained in her path. Fluffy, however, seemed to have no idea of how badly she had behaved and jumped around, barking happily.

Esther Mueller's dog, Rumpelstiltskin, having pulled off every last shred of his ridiculous outfit, performed well and was currently in third place. The dog was so diminutive he could hardly have knocked over an obstacle if he tried. He was, however, unusually slow and deliberate and paused incessantly to think about what he was doing. A panel of judges chosen from the small pool of middle school honor students scribbled away. They held their results up high above their heads. Accuracy: nine. Speed: two and a half. Thomas breathed a sigh of relief.

Stuart Seltzer's beagle, Franklin, surprised everyone. The dog might have had a real shot at top honors except for the fact that Stuart became overly excited during the race and had to suddenly leave to go to the bathroom.

Much to no one's surprise, Ralph Sidell and Willie performed quite well and were currently in first place. McGrowl wasn't impressed. He felt that Willie gave a capable but nonetheless lackluster performance.

"McGrowlll is a three-year-olddd goldennn retriever that enjoys chasing catsss and loves mashed potatoesss and Chinese fooddd."

Adrenaline began to course through McGrowl's highly advanced neurosystem. Every muscle in his body stood poised and ready to spring into action. Thomas could feel the butterflies forming in his stomach as he and the dog moved swiftly forward to take their places. "We can do it, we can do it," Thomas said to himself. McGrowl looked up at the boy and nodded his head in resolute agreement.

All eyes were on the dog and Thomas. Suddenly, without warning, the dog sensed something and let out an involuntary growl. Only McGrowl could have heard it, but a noise that sounded an awful lot like purring was coming from somewhere in the crowd.

"What's happening?" Thomas whispered under his breath.

McGrowl told Thomas not to worry, but Thomas knew something was definitely the matter. "Easy boy, steady now." He gave the dog a reassuring pat.

"On your mark, get set, go!" A whistle blew and a flag was waved. McGrowl didn't budge.

His ears started twitching, and his nose caught the unmistakably familiar scent. His super-vision confirmed the diagnosis: cat in the area, cat in the area. Every one of his magnificent senses cried out in complete agreement. His knees grew weak, and he practically stumbled over his own paws as he glanced over at the source of his irritation. A buzz of curious whispering rippled throughout the excited crowd. What was happening? The clock was ticking, and precious seconds were being lost.

The cat from next door stared out contentedly from her vantage point at the front of the field. She had heard the dogs barking and Principal Grimble's bullhorn and had wandered over to the field to see what was going on. She was nothing if not curious. She waved her aggravating tail around as she groomed herself lazily. Occasionally, she swatted at a fly. She purred contentedly. McGrowl would chase her. He would catch her. He would teach her a lesson she would never forget.

The images came roaring into Thomas's head. "Don't even think about it," Thomas said tersely as he urged McGrowl forward. The purring grew louder. The dog concentrated with all his might and gritted his teeth. The purring began to subside a little. The last thing he wanted to do was disappoint the boy. "Please, McGrowl." Thomas was desperate.

A hush fell over the crowd. The clock was still running. Thomas and McGrowl were at a complete standstill. Violet bit her lip and tried to send McGrowl a telepathic message. She was, of course, unsuccessful. The dog thought about how much he wanted to win. He thought about how much he loved Thomas. And then he thought about mashed potatoes.

The purring subsided, and McGrowl

breathed a sigh of relief. *Good boy,* Thomas thought. *Let's get going.*

McGrowl started forward. He wound his way around the first series of obstacles without a hitch, but Thomas could tell the dog was still a little shaky. He wasn't running with the speed that Thomas knew he was capable of, and he slipped on a particularly difficult turn. The crowd held their breath as the dog skidded and nearly collided into a row of carefully arranged milk bottles. He had practiced that turn so many times he could make it in his sleep. The presence of the cat had so shaken him, it now took every ounce of his concentration to remain on all four paws.

Lewis Musser was beside himself with happiness. Spike barked cheerfully, and Lewis's parents nudged themselves smugly and whispered excitedly about what they described as "McGrowl's decidedly mediocre performance."

Thomas kept sending the dog encouraging messages. By the end of the course McGrowl was doing a little better. But clearly the dog's confidence had suffered a severe blow. McGrowl sent so many *I'm sorry* messages that Thomas had to restrain himself from leaning over and giving the dog a big hug. He didn't want to embarrass him, and besides, stopping and hugging your pet during a timed event was never a good idea.

When they made it past the finish line, the crowd applauded tepidly, and both Thomas and the dog listened anxiously to find out whether they had even qualified.

The judges scribbled and jotted on their notepads and whispered to one another intensely. And then they handed their decision over to Principal Grimble, who held up his bullhorn and paused for dramatic effect. "First to qualify" — he looked over at the judges — "drumroll please, Miss Thompson."

The teacher looked back at Principal Grimble as if he were out of his mind. "Lewisss Musser's dog, Spike." Everyone applauded loudly.

Ralph Sidell and Willie came in second. The crowd roared. McGrowl listened anxiously. "Third place wouldn't be that bad," he consoled himself.

He whined miserably when he heard Principal Grimble's booming voice. "And congratulations are in order to Stuart Seltzer and Franklin for placing thirddd."

Thomas softly reminded him that no matter what, McGrowl would always be first in his heart. McGrowl looked up at the boy gratefully but had to admit he didn't feel all that much better. When McGrowl heard Principal Grimble announce that Rumpelstiltskin the Chihuahua was in fourth place, he held his paws over his ears and hung his head. "And fifth but not leasttt," Principal Grimble an-

nounced proudly, "Thomasss and McGrowlll."
If dogs could blush, he would have blushed
with shame.

A smattering of polite applause arose from
the crowd, and then all five qualifying finalists
lined up on the platform to accept their certifi-
cates of commendation.

"Thank you, childrennn. Thankkk you,
dogsss. Thank you, weather, for cooperat-
inggg. Don't forgettt to sign out with your
homerooms before you get on your busessss."
Principal Grimble took a deep breath and
smiled broadly. "The Big Dog Show is in two
weeksss. To each and every one of our de-
lightful canine competitorsss, I have only one
thing to say." He paused dramatically. "May
the fursss be with you."

A groan went up from the disbanding
crowd. As much as everyone hated Principal
Grimble's jokes, they hated his puns even
more.

McGrowl, Thomas, and Violet headed for home. "What happened to McGrowl today?" Violet wondered.

"He doesn't like cats," Thomas answered. "It's a problem."

"So I gathered." Violet picked up a white-tufted dandelion and blew on it gently. "Can't you do anything about it? Like desensitizing exercises or something?" Spidery little seedlings floated in the air.

"We're working on it," Thomas replied. McGrowl walked beside Thomas and Violet with his head held low. He wasn't feeling very good about himself. He had wanted so badly to be a good dog.

"I know how hard you tried, and that's all that counts," Thomas said gently. "We'll do better next time, I know we will." McGrowl gave Thomas a mournful look. Violet glanced over sympathetically. She could imagine how badly McGrowl felt. If Sophie Morris's dog,

Fluffy, had done one tiny bit better, McGrowl wouldn't even have qualified.

Next time, McGrowl thought, *I will make Thomas so proud of me.* He was determined to win. Nothing would stand in his way.

They arrived at Thomas's house, and everyone stared at the caravan of shiny black limousines stationed in the driveway. An impressive visitor had come to call on Thomas and his family. And Thomas had a feeling he knew exactly who it was.

CHAPTER SEVEN
Dog in the Hood

"Don't burn your tongues on the pigs-in-blankets. They're extremely hot." Mrs. Wiggins was scurrying around the living room, offering a tray of delicious little hot dogs. Everyone concurred that getting burned by hot food was about the most horrible thing that could happen to anyone.

Mel Muchnick, the Wiggins's impressive surprise visitor, joined in the chorus. "Got a burn from a fried mozzarella stick two years ago I'll never forget. Nothing more lethal than hot cheese." This didn't deter him from picking up a handful of steaming mini wieners and stuffing them into his mouth.

Mr. Wiggins nodded in enthusiastic agreement. He was too excited to actually speak. Never in his life did he imagine that a real live mayoral candidate and his glamorous fiancée would be sitting in his very own living room. The presence of such exalted visitors made even the normally terrifying Mr. and Mrs. Lundquist seem about as threatening as a pair of comfortable old shoes.

"What I want to know is how you managed to squeeze those plump little wieners into their tiny little wrappers?" As Mel Muchnick spoke he shoveled pigs-in-blankets into his mouth so fast his hands were practically a blur. His fiancée, Lily Von Vleck, kept handing him napkins. She dabbed at the ketchup that dribbled down Muchnick's chin and threatened to land on Mrs. Wiggins's brand-new white wall-to-wall carpeting.

"Ve must learn ze control of ze appetite, Mel, darlink." Miss Von Vleck spoke with a German accent that was almost as heavy as her makeup. Her eyelashes fluttered about like giant moths, and her bulging lips maintained a glossy purplish veneer that seemed impervious to food or drink of any kind. She wore a slinky blue dress with so many sequins Thomas had to shield his eyes from the glare with his hand.

Her *w*'s sounded like *v*'s, and everything else in between sounded as if she were speaking with a mouthful of marbles. At first Thomas thought she was speaking in German. Then he managed to decipher one or two of her badly mangled phrases and decided she simply had the strongest accent he had ever heard — but she was, indeed, speaking English.

"Horsepucky, Lily, my dear!" Muchnick exclaimed. Unfortunately, his mouth was so full of ketchup and pigs-in-blankets that a thick glob of Heinz's best came flying out along with his words. It made a graceful arc and landed right in the middle of the rug.

Everyone stared in horror at the offending red condiment. No one dared speak until Mrs. Wiggins broke the silence with a jolly, "Oh, who cares about that silly old rug? I was thinking of throwing it away anyway." And with that, she picked up a pig-in-blanket herself, poured ketchup all over it, and threw it onto the rug next to Muchnick's. "So there!"

She turned on her heels and rushed into the kitchen to get some more spinach triangles.

Thomas alone could see her biting her lip to keep from sobbing. *People sure act funny around mayoral candidates,* he observed silently.

Over an assortment of crab-laden crackers artfully arranged to spell out WIN WITH MEL, the candidate and his fiancée began laying out their strategy. "Loved the parade, but it's not enough," said Muchnick. Lily picked up the ball and ran with it. "Vat vee mean to zay is dat vee vant more of dat publicity stuff, hokeydokey?"

"Can't understand a word she says, but she sure is a cutie." Mel Muchnick gave his fiancée an adoring smile and an affectionate pat on the shoulder. Lily Von Vleck gave him a playful smack on the wrist and attempted to remove an entire half of a chicken that Muchnick was cramming into his mouth. "Don't vant to appear fet on da television shoes." Thomas quickly determined that *fet* meant fat, but it took him a moment to convert *television shoes* into television shows.

Meanwhile, Mel held on to the chicken for dear life, and for several tense moments the two of them wrestled with the charbroiled fowl with all their might. Being the stronger of the two, Muchnick eventually won the tug-of-war, but by now the poor chicken resembled a limp dishrag more than a tasty main dish.

Mr. Lundquist was anxious to return to the subject at hand. "But what about the commercial?"

"Like the commercial, don't love it," Muchnick responded tersely. Thomas could see the fear and apprehension in his father's eyes. Lily lowered her already husky voice a couple of octaves and purred in her velvety growl, "Ve feel it could use more, ow you say — poomph."

"I believe that's oomph, sugarplum, and I agree," Muchnick said as he hurled a cheese ball over in the direction of his beloved. Lily Von Vleck quickly opened her enormous mouth and snapped at the hors d'oeuvre, catching it effortlessly between her startlingly white teeth. Thomas was instantly reminded of the sea lions at the zoo at feeding time.

Mrs. and Mrs. Lundquist applauded loudly. "Bravo," they yelled as Lily took a series of quick little bows.

Mrs. Wiggins waltzed back into the room and passed out more bite-sized spinach triangles. She pretended to drop a paper napkin on the floor near the ketchup stain. As she bent down to pick it up she frantically rubbed at the red blotch with a solution of vinegar and egg whites that she kept for just such occasions.

Muchnick didn't even notice. He was completely wrapped up in what he was describing as "the television commercial of the century." He stood up and gestured extravagantly as he continued. "None of that fancy political stuff. Nobody cares about politics. Human interest's what we want, know what I mean?"

"Vell put, Mel, sveetie," Lily exclaimed, and jumped up and down excitedly. Thomas observed that her hair had been so heavily lacquered that even violent jumping didn't disturb a single strand.

Mr. Wiggins finally found his voice. "You mean throw out the whole thing?" His lower lip quivered with disappointment. He had stayed up for the last twenty-four hours creating what he felt were perfect scenarios.

"You bet your sweet bippie," Muchnick replied. "I'm thinking something simple. Something direct. Say, a small boy playing with his dog and talking to the camera. Say, someone like young Thomas, here. And for the dog we get — oh, I don't know — that dog we saw at the parade yesterday."

"I'm not sure what dog you're referring to," Mr. Wiggins ventured innocently. But, of course, he knew exactly what dog Muchnick was talking about.

"You know," Muchnick continued, "the retriever. Real cute. Cuddly. Adorable brown eyes. Obedient. Good-natured. Smart. I want that dog, Wiggins, and I want it now."

A loud, insistent thumping began. It echoed throughout the room and shook the house. Everyone looked about nervously. Thomas realized instantly what was happening. McGrowl had heard every word of the conversation in the living room with his superhearing. His powerful tail was wagging joyously and uncontrollably against the floorboards in response to the lavish praise he was receiving.

McGrowl could restrain himself no longer and came hurtling down the stairs to receive his compliments in person. Mr. Wiggins crept carefully but quickly to an open window and was prepared to jump in case the dog made a move for him.

Mr. Muchnick smiled broadly. "Quick work, Wiggins." Muchnick ran right over and offered McGrowl a plate of assorted hors d'oeuvres.

The dog ate as quickly as Muchnick, only a lot more neatly.

As excited as he was to be receiving treats, he noticed something familiar about Muchnick's scent. He had noticed it before. He knew he would place it eventually. His nose never failed him.

The Von Vleck woman smelled familiar, too. But every time he got close enough to get a good sniff, the woman found an excuse to move away.

By the end of the evening an entire television commercial starring Thomas and McGrowl had been carefully designed. Mr. Wiggins offered helpful suggestions from the far side of the room. He pretended he had an allergy and had to remain near an open window.

It was quickly determined that the commercial would focus on Muchnick's honesty and his forceful stand against crime. This new wave of robberies had everybody more than a little concerned.

They all agreed that the incumbent mayor, Stanley Fitch, was a lazy old coot and appeared to be doing little to remedy the situation. His complacent attitude was costing him precious votes.

"Sniff out crime" was selected as the new campaign slogan. Mr. Wiggins proudly accepted congratulations for that brilliant contribution. The commercial would end with McGrowl demonstrating his remarkable ability to sniff on cue and Thomas looking into the camera and praising Muchnick's ten-point program to stamp out crime.

McGrowl was sent upstairs. Mr. Wiggins was able to leave his post by the window, and all three Wigginses bade good-bye to their illustrious guests.

As Mr. and Mrs. Wiggins headed for the kitchen to begin the nightly cleanup, Thomas thought about his big day tomorrow. The minute school was over, the boy and his dog would be picked up by a limousine and rushed to a television studio to begin filming the commercial.

Both Wiggins parents were so wrapped up in their own thoughts that neither noticed the little drawer in the kitchen standing half open. Mrs. Wiggins kept a few spare dollars there for tipping deliverymen. The drawer had been ransacked, and the money was nowhere to be seen.

As Thomas walked past the living room and toward the winding staircase that led upstairs, he noticed a small silver toothpick with the initials MM on it. Evidently, the illustrious visitor had dropped it sometime during his frenzy of eating. Thomas put it in his pocket.

When Thomas pulled up the covers and turned out the glowing rocket-shaped lamp that burned brightly by his bedside, McGrowl stared out the window, lost in thought. "Come to bed, it's really late," the boy said as sleep overcame him and his head sank into his pillow. But the dog just sat and stared.

He didn't want to say anything to Thomas yet because he wasn't one hundred percent certain, and he didn't want to cause the boy a sleepless night. But he was pretty sure he had recognized the odor he had detected. Why hadn't he realized it the moment he had first noticed it at the parade?

Lurking beneath the musk and penetrating fumes of Muchnick's cologne, there lingered a hint of formaldehyde, the telltale scent of the evil stranger. Could there possibly be some connection between Muchnick and the forces of evil McGrowl had grown to dislike so intensely? He hoped he was mistaken. He wouldn't rest until he knew for sure. Until then, he wouldn't leave the boy's side for a second.

A little shiver of fear tingled at the back of McGrowl's neck as he moved closer to the bed and positioned himself between the boy and the door. Thomas was snoring gently and innocently. A grim look of determination came over the dog's usually peaceful face as he hunkered down for a long and sleepless night.

CHAPTER EIGHT
Sherlock Bones

"Why do we have to get there so early?" Violet asked groggily. She couldn't understand why Thomas and McGrowl had shown up forty minutes ahead of schedule and insisted on leaving for school at such a ridiculously early time. "No one's even gonna be there."

"We've gotta work on our science project, remember, and the lab's booked the rest of the day," Thomas lied. Violet's mother, Mrs. Schnayerson, looked over proudly. She took great pleasure in Violet's scientific achievements.

"I thought we finished that project last —" But before Violet could finish her sentence Thomas gave her a deliberate nudge with his foot, and Violet finally got the point. She continued seamlessly. "Oh, yes, I remember now. We have to redo that part where the hydrogen combines with the nitrogen and causes matriculation."

Fortunately, Mrs. Schnayerson knew absolutely nothing about science or she would have realized that Violet was uttering sheer nonsense. Thomas was up to something and didn't want Violet's mom to know about it.

Mrs. Schnayerson finished whipping up a fluffernutter sandwich and tucked it into Violet's lunch bag along with a cream puff and some barbecued potato chips. Thomas's mouth practically watered. His mother always insisted on putting together a lunch box according to the latest nutritional guidelines. She wouldn't have dreamed of including a single item from Violet's delicious menu.

McGrowl whined so sadly that Mrs. Schnayerson made him his very own fluffer-nutter, which he managed to consume in a single gulp. He would spend the rest of the morning licking marshmallow fluff from every single one of his white-coated whiskers. "Good luck on that science project, kids," Mrs. Schnayerson called as the three friends hurried off to catch the seven-thirty bus.

In spite of Violet's pleas, Thomas refused to explain the highly secret nature of their mission until the three of them were all alone in the school yard. Mr. Postino, the school custodian, had let them in the front door. Thomas often showed up early to finish an assignment, so Mr. Postino didn't evince the slightest suspicion.

"Let's start in homeroom," Thomas whispered as he rushed down the hall to the empty classroom. "Whoever broke into Miss Rabkin's office was probably the same person who stole from the treasury. And we're gonna look for clues."

"What kind of clues?" Violet asked in a hushed tone. There was nothing she loved more than a good mystery.

"Don't know. But a criminal always leaves behind some kind of evidence. Haven't you ever read Sherlock Holmes?"

"Oh, yeah. Sure. Of course," Violet replied confidently. She had never even heard of the man, but she wasn't about to admit it.

Thomas had recently finished a thrilling adventure story about the brilliant British detective. There was no crime Holmes and his trusted assistant, Doctor Watson, couldn't solve. Thomas couldn't see why he and Violet couldn't solve any crime, either. Especially with the help of McGrowl.

By now they had arrived at their homeroom

only to discover that the door was locked. As McGrowl hunted around for a long pointy object with which to pick the lock, Thomas whispered excitedly into Violet's ear. "I've got a hunch the same person who stole the class treasury may have broken into Miss Rabkin's room, and I wanna gather incriminating evidence. That's what Holmes always does."

The sound of footsteps rounding the corner caused both children to drop abruptly to the floor and pretend to be playing a game of marbles. "Science lab's in the other direction, kids," Mr. Postino reminded them.

"Thanks, Mr. P," Thomas answered. "Just want to finish up this game of marbles and then we'll be on our way." Thomas leaned over his imaginary shooter and tried to block as much of the supposed "marbles" as he could. Mr. Postino was pretty nearsighted, and chances were good that he wouldn't notice there was not a single marble there.

"Say, mind if I join in? I used to be a pretty good marbles player when I was a kid." Mr. Postino leaned over and was about to discover Thomas's ploy.

"That's great, Mr. P, except Violet and I are getting over terrible coughs, and we wouldn't want you to get sick." Thomas remembered that Mr. Postino was something of a hypochondriac. Both he and Violet started coughing violently. The lanky custodian backed away quickly.

"Thanks for the warning, kids; can't afford to get sick. Not with Thanksgiving coming up." Mr. Postino hurried off, and Thomas and Violet continued to cough for a couple of extra seconds just to make sure he wouldn't return.

Meanwhile, McGrowl had located a hairpin on the floor and came bounding over to the children. No doubt it came from the severe gray bun that sat imperiously on the top of Miss Thompson's pointy head.

"Thanks," Thomas said as he took the long, skinny object and started fiddling around with the lock. McGrowl let Thomas attempt to pick the lock for a couple of minutes and then gently nudged him away, took the hairpin carefully in his mouth, and had the door open in two seconds.

"Good work, Dr. Watson," Thomas said as he scratched the dog behind his ears. He and Violet walked slowly into the room while McGrowl stood guard.

"First of all, we've gotta be really careful not to touch anything. We might disturb a clue, like a fingerprint or something," Thomas warned.

"But how will we ever uncover any clues if we don't touch anything?" Violet asked somewhat impatiently.

"If we find something we'll put on plastic gloves and handle the clue as little as possible." Thomas held up a pair of the disposable hand guards his mother insisted everybody wear whenever raw chicken or meat was being prepared.

"I think I see something," Violet said with more urgency than was necessary. She spotted a pen that had fallen onto the floor. She leaned over and examined it with great care. At last she spoke. "It's mine. I lost it yesterday." She picked it up and put it into her pocket.

"Look. Over here," Thomas whispered. Mr. Postino had neglected to clean up a small pile of chalk dust in the corner near the blackboard.

"What is it?" Violet asked, and peered down at the little white pile.

"I think we found ourselves a clue," Thomas said as matter-of-factly as he could manage. His heart was racing. Violet leaned over to look, and the chalk dust tickled her nose so violently she almost sneezed. She summoned up all the restraint she could muster and stifled the potentially evidence-destroying gesture.

"What do we do now?" Violet asked. She pulled out a tissue and blew her nose as hard as she could.

"We call in the big guns," Thomas said. He nodded at McGrowl, and the dog came trotting over to investigate.

"I'll stand guard," Violet said, and changed places with McGrowl.

McGrowl focused his laserlike vision on the exciting clue. As the dog stared and concentrated with all his might, a series of swirling wavy lines imbedded in the chalk came into sharper and clearer focus.

McGrowl's eyes were functioning with the precision and acuity of a powerful electron microscope. Fingerprints embedded in the dust came into view. McGrowl took a picture with his mind. The dog had a photographic memory. Anything he saw even once became instantly and permanently embedded in his brain cells. He was, in effect, a walking digital camera — a camera with an endless supply of film and the finest lens that no amount of money could ever buy: a dog's eye.

"I think he's onto something. Something big," Thomas said eagerly. The two children ran to catch up with McGrowl, who was heading straight for Mabel Rabkin's office. The children were so excited they didn't notice it was almost eight-twenty and the bell for first period was about to ring. In two minutes, several hundred noisy students and teachers would come barreling down the hallways and into their classrooms.

CHAPTER NINE
The Plot Thickens

McGrowl, Thomas, and Violet were carefully sifting through clues in Miss Rabkin's office when the bell rang, accompanied by the clatter of approaching feet. Violet poked her head out the door and spotted the woman ambling slowly toward her office.

"Quick, she's almost here. We gotta get out," Violet whispered urgently.

"We need another minute," Thomas replied. "By tomorrow there won't be a single clue left intact. Stall her."

"What am I supposed to do?" Violet asked somewhat desperately.

"You're smart. Think of something," Thomas said as he resumed his search.

Violet ran out of the office and fell to the floor, writhing in pain in the middle of the corridor.

"What's the matter, honey?" Miss Rabkin inquired.

"I was skipping rope and I wrenched my ankle."

Miss Rabkin dropped quickly to the floor with more speed than Violet would have thought the eighty-year-old woman capable of. "Let's have a look."

"I thought maybe you could help me get to Nurse Boynton's office," Violet said weakly. Ever the quick thinker, she had realized that the nurse's office was on the second floor. By the time Miss Rabkin accompanied her there,

Thomas and McGrowl would have had plenty of time to complete their search.

"No need," Miss Rabkin said cheerfully. "I've recently completed my CPR recertification, and there's nothing I can't handle in the way of a small emergency." And then she pulled out a little bag filled with splints, tape, and an assortment of bandages and started working away. Violet pretended she was in great pain and tried to make it as difficult as possible for Miss Rabkin to move her supposedly injured ankle.

Meanwhile, Thomas and McGrowl searched frantically. Miss Rabkin was obsessively clean and had already removed any traces of dust or debris that Mr. Postino might have left behind when he cleaned up at the end of the day. There wasn't a clue in sight.

Finally, McGrowl noticed something. Wedged halfway between the window and a small built-in bookcase, the tiniest piece of a torn file stuck out unobtrusively. No one but Mc-Growl would have ever noticed it.

Using his superpower mental strength, Mc-Growl quickly enlarged and memorized the one fingerprint that he could find. The scrap of paper was tiny and actually contained only a small portion of the complete print. It was enough, however, for McGrowl to quickly determine that the print indeed was made by the same person who had entered both rooms the day of the break-ins. Chances were good that if the fingerprint's owner could be located, the crimes would be solved.

"Good work, boy," Thomas said proudly. He put on his plastic gloves and looked closely at the scrap of paper. All he could make out were the letters "Iton S." The larger piece of paper from which the scrap had been torn was likely to contain the remaining letters — and the answer to the mystery.

As Thomas and McGrowl pondered the clue, they failed to notice a pair of beady little eyes peering in at them from the window behind Mabel Rabkin's desk. The eyes darted back and forth a couple of times and then quickly disappeared beneath the window ledge. They belonged to none other than Mel Muchnick, who, in order to get a better look into the office, was standing somewhat shakily on the delicate shoulders of Lily Von Vleck.

"Good-bye, Miss Rabkin." Violet was practically shouting now.

Miss Rabkin seemed a little miffed. "For heaven's sake, I'm old, but I'm not deaf."

Thomas got the point. He and McGrowl were out of that office like a shot and halfway down the corridor before they realized they had left Violet behind. "Wait for me," she called out, and forgetting about her wrenched ankle, ran off after them.

"Take it easy, dear, or I'll send you to the infirmary," Miss Rabkin announced firmly before walking into her office and shutting the door at last.

As they hurried back to homeroom, Violet tripped on a combination lock someone had carelessly left in the middle of the hallway. She hurtled to the ground and landed with a giant splat.

The first thing she saw when she opened her eyes was a little silver object lying on the floor directly in front of her. McGrowl immediately sniffed it and began to growl. And then Thomas picked it up and realized why. It was a little sterling silver toothpick, and it had the initials MM on it. It was identical to the toothpick Muchnick had dropped at Thomas's house last night.

And then the bell rang and children began to stampede through the hall like a herd of wild buffalo.

But what did the letters "lton S" have to do

with anything? And why would a respected mayoral candidate go to the trouble of stealing money from small children and breaking into a kindly old registrar's office?

All three young detectives pondered these and other questions as Lewis Musser swaggered over. He told Thomas and Violet they would have to get him something really special for lunch today if they ever hoped to get off his list. "I'm thinking doughnuts. I'm thinking devil's food cake. I'm thinking 'surprise me.'"

McGrowl was so upset with the unfairness of Lewis's request that he had to restrain himself from taking a bite out of one of the boy's beefy legs. But he knew it was the wrong thing to do, and anyway, Thomas was in enough trouble as it was.

And then Lewis turned on his heels and ran off to chase after Janie Mingenbach, the prettiest girl in the entire middle school. Janie had absolutely no interest in Lewis. She liked older boys, and actually had her sights set on Thomas's brother, Roger. She didn't seem to care that everybody knew Roger was absolutely one hundred percent devoted to Violet's older sister, Alicia.

At this moment Roger was busy carrying Alicia's books from one class to the next. Alicia pretended she had strained her hand in a sewing accident and needed a big strong boy to help her out. Thomas and Violet saw right through her tired old ploy, but Roger fell for it hook, line, and sinker. Thomas hoped he wouldn't lose all of his senses when he reached sixteen.

All day Thomas and Violet passed notes back and forth. Miss Thompson caught them twice, and they were almost sent to the principal's office. But Violet pretended her ankle was still bothering her and pleaded for leniency, which she got.

IT'S A DOG'S LIFE

During recess, Thomas and Violet huddled together by the drinking fountain and decided that Thomas would show up at the commercial as scheduled, and Violet would accompany him. They didn't want Muchnick to suspect they were onto his dirty tricks. Thomas decided against returning the silver toothpicks.

McGrowl raided lunch boxes when no one was looking and managed to assemble enough good stuff to keep Lewis from hurting anybody. He replaced the missing candies and cookies with quarters he was able to find by searching the parking lot behind the school.

Thomas couldn't imagine how they would ever convince anybody of Muchnick's guilt. They had evidence, but it was circumstantial at best. Thomas knew the entire case rested on the talents of a bionic dog that communicated his results telepathically.

They decided then and there they would

have to catch Muchnick and his assistant in the act. McGrowl stayed especially close to both children. The dog was sure of one thing. Whoever Mel Muchnick was, he wasn't what he seemed. And that wasn't good.

CHAPTER TEN
Fame

Lily Von Vleck was beside herself with joy. Mel Muchnick had broken down and let her be in the commercial. She would play the role of the kindly stranger who gets robbed. When she learned the news she cried so hard she had to spend several hours in makeup repairing her face. "Vatch de lashes, dollink, der da last vons I got," she warned the nervous makeup woman.

Mr. Wiggins ran around issuing orders and writing on a clipboard he clung to as if it were a life raft. Meanwhile, Muchnick sat in a corner, learning his lines and muttering to himself. He knew how important the commercial was to his campaign and wanted to make sure everything went perfectly.

Mr. Wiggins had sent for an acting coach all the way from St. Louis. Larry La Rue, as the man was known, had already confused Muchnick severely by telling him he didn't find him one bit sincere. He convinced the anxious candidate that unless he could cry real tears during his big speech at the end of the commercial, absolutely no one would ever vote for him.

He gave Muchnick a list of sad things to think about and then went ahead and upset Miss Von Vleck by telling her he didn't find her wholesome enough to play her part and asking her if she could do anything about her image. He might as well have asked a giraffe to get shorter as to have asked Lily to appear more wholesome.

IT'S A DOG'S LIFE

And then Thomas and Violet and McGrowl arrived. The limousine had picked them up exactly on time, and everything was going smoothly. It did take a little effort to convince the driver that McGrowl was supposed to ride with them in the back of the shiny black Mercedes stretch.

The driver attempted to get McGrowl into the front seat at first, but the dog leaped to the roof of the car and refused to come down until Thomas assured him he could ride in the back with Violet and himself. The dog had never ridden in a limousine before and had been looking forward to it the entire day.

McGrowl enjoyed the ride tremendously. By the time they arrived at the studio he had polished off all of the gum and candy he found hidden away in the little pockets beside the armrests.

From the moment he entered the studio, McGrowl didn't take his eyes off Muchnick.

Mr. Wiggins didn't take his eyes off McGrowl and thought up excuses to leave the room whenever possible.

Muchnick immediately noticed something was bothering the normally cheerful animal. "Where's that old sparkle and verve, kids? We're counting on the pooch to win us a lot of votes. He looks about as happy as a mermaid in a snowstorm."

It was decided that Violet would play the silent but important role of Thomas's friend. McGrowl was given a slouchy hat to wear and a pipe. The dog strutted up and down the room, clenching the pipe in his mouth precisely the way he had seen Sherlock do on the cover of *The Hound of the Baskervilles.*

"He's a better actor than everybody in this room combined," La Rue announced loudly. Miss Von Vleck began to cry again until Muchnick reminded her she didn't have any more eyelashes left. McGrowl pretended to sniff at everyone as if he were a great doggy detective. Which, of course, he was.

"That dog possesses a raw animal instinct that's rare even among animals." La Rue got down on his hands and knees and held out a stale piece of bread to show his appreciation. McGrowl turned up his nose and headed in the opposite direction.

"Places, please. The commercial is about to begin," a voice called from inside the studio. Everyone hurried into the staging area and noticed Mr. Wiggins standing on top of a pile of scenery as if it were the only spot from which to direct an important commercial. He was, of course, placing himself as far away from McGrowl as he could without anyone noticing.

"Last looks, everyone," he shouted. Wiggins had spent some time observing how professional filmmakers worked and knew that before you rolled any film you had to shout the phrase "last looks." This was the signal for all the makeup and hair people to come rushing out and add a little extra powder or pat down a strand of unruly hair before the filming began.

Not wishing to appear stupid or uninformed, everyone simply looked as long and as hard as they could at everyone else, as if it were indeed the last time they would ever be looking at them.

Lily Von Vleck got so sad thinking it was the last time she would be looking at Mel Muchnick that she started to cry again, completely destroying her third and last pair of false eyelashes. She had to complete the filming with no eyelashes whatsoever. Larry La Rue actually said the no-eyelash look helped her to appear more wholesome.

"Lights, camera, action!" Wiggins yelled. Thomas took his place on the set and started speaking his lines. McGrowl had helped him practice, and he knew them perfectly.

"There's been a lot of crime in Cedar Springs lately," Thomas began. All of a sudden Lily Von Vleck's voice drowned out Thomas's. "Vat's my line? *Gott in Himmel*, I vorgot my line," she called out hysterically. Larry La Rue ran over to her and began frantically whispering.

"Cut," Mr. Wiggins yelled. "Is there a problem?"

"It's like this, Mr. Wiggins," Larry La Rue began. "I believe Miss Von Vleck has forgotten her motivation."

"Her what?" Muchnick roared.

"Her motivation. The thing that is causing her to say her line. She has forgotten why she is saying her line, and therefore she has forgotten the line itself."

It suddenly became very still on the set.

And then Mr. Muchnick got highly agitated and started screaming. "Here's your motivation: She either says her line or the two of you will be out of here on your keesters so fast your heads will be swimming."

Thomas had never heard the word *keester* before, but evidently it provided sufficient motivation, because the rest of the commercial went extremely smoothly. From that point on, no one seemed to forget anything or make even the smallest of mistakes.

"What's a keester?" the boy whispered to his friend.

"I'm not sure, but I think it's something you sit on," Violet replied under her breath.

McGrowl behaved impressively. He sniffed on cue and never once dropped his pipe or attempted to remove his hat.

Lily Von Vleck made her brief appearance as a crime victim and said her line, "Please, on behalf of all crime victims, elect Muchnick," without a hitch.

Mel Muchnick himself performed magnificently. He came out at the end of the commercial and explained how much he loved Cedar Springs and how much ridding the little town of crime meant to him. He simply thought about how upset he would be if he weren't elected and cried right on cue. La Rue was so impressed he nearly applauded and ruined the take.

When it was time for everyone to go home Mr. Wiggins yelled, "That's a wrap," and Muchnick pulled out a bottle of champagne and toasted everyone.

Whatever happens, McGrowl thought, *the man mustn't be elected mayor.* The consequences for the little town could be disastrous. But what could McGrowl do? Who would ever believe him? And if Muchnick didn't get elected, would Mr. Wiggins lose his job? What a terrible predicament!

Thomas tried to pretend he wasn't receiving every single worrisome thought from McGrowl. But he was, and as he and Violet said good-bye to everyone, Thomas had to struggle to appear unconcerned. The performance was far more challenging than the one he had just completed in the commercial.

Mr. Wiggins took Thomas aside and congratulated him on a job well done. And then he looked his son in the eye, long and hard.

"I want you to tell the dog he did well, too. This does not mean I like him," he was quick to add. "But he did a good job, and it's not his fault he was born a canine." McGrowl listened quietly from a distant corner and gave himself a little pat on the back.

Thomas and Violet and McGrowl trudged over to the bus station. Evidently, limousines took you to commercials, but they didn't drive you home afterward. The three friends were celebrities no longer. They were happy to return to real life, except for the fact that they had an extremely serious situation on their hands. And none of them had the slightest idea what they were going to do about it.

CHAPTER ELEVEN
Night Crawlers

During the days that preceded the Big Dog Show, Thomas and McGrowl practiced a series of complicated maneuvers. Violet held up pictures of cats in an attempt to distract McGrowl. Once she even brought over an extremely realistic cat puppet. She had given it to her Aunt Sadie's pet Siamese kitten, so the puppet even smelled like the real thing.

McGrowl passed the test beautifully. He didn't exhibit the slightest interest. Even when Violet operated the puppet with great skill, McGrowl looked over scornfully and continued walking on his rear paws without a hitch. It seemed unlikely that a real cat would be able to distract McGrowl tonight. Even Mrs. Wiggins confessed she thought McGrowl's pet trick was first-rate.

Every other spare moment was spent trying to catch Muchnick and Von Vleck in the act. Certainly there had been plenty of opportunities. The robberies in town continued unabated. No store or house was safe. It seemed everybody was missing a piggy bank or an antique clock or a brand-new pair of shoes.

Incumbent mayor Stanley Fitch was sinking lower and lower in the polls. Poor Officer Nelson didn't seem to be any closer to finding the culprits than he had been the week before. He was considering turning in his badge and returning to his first love, supermarket management.

It seemed as if Muchnick's tough stand on crime was a winning ticket to a certain landslide on election day. Mr. Wiggins's commercial played continually. Everywhere Thomas and McGrowl went, cars honked and passersby waved enthusiastically. They were celebrities. The local candy store proudly announced that McGrowl preferred their brand of fudge to any other. They even decided to name the peanut-and-marshmallow concoction the dog loved after him. They called it McFudge.

Poor Thomas felt helpless. Try though they might, Muchnick and Von Vleck always seemed to be one step ahead of the boy and his dog. Today would be different. Thomas and Violet and McGrowl would root out corruption and banish the evil duo once and for all. They had to. If they didn't, Muchnick would soon be elected mayor, and nothing and no one would be able to stand in his way.

Unbeknownst to Thomas, Muchnick and Von Vleck had noticed the youngsters and their dog snooping about after them one afternoon. They knew the children were onto them and so they devised a wicked plan. A simple plan. They would remove Thomas and Violet from the picture. And McGrowl? They would capture the dog and force him to join them in their quest to destroy Cedar Springs.

"Where do you think you're going, young man?" Mrs. Wiggins said as she finished shampooing the rug. She had moved the furniture around until it formed a perfect semicircle around the center of the living room, the place where the ugly red stain had been. Thomas was reminded of the early settlers and their covered wagons, clustered around a blazing fire.

Mrs. Wiggins's second cousin, Tweedy Dry, way over in Wappinger's Falls, was missing a series of collectible china plates depicting scenes from *Lost in Space*. Mrs. Wiggins's guard was definitely up.

"Shouldn't you be rehearsing your pet trick?" she asked rather pointedly.

"Gotta go see Violet about a big paper we're doing on" — he paused — "Thomas Edison and the combustion engine."

His mother stopped what she was doing and looked up at him solemnly. "Make sure you're back in plenty of time to bathe and dress for your big event. I am so excited. I'll be on pins and needles if you're a second late."

"No problem," Thomas replied cheerfully, and stole a glance at his watch. He was already late for Violet. He had two hours to save the world and get to the dog show.

"I'm picking up your father at the office. We'll meet you at school at six-thirty." She leaned over to check the boy's shirt for ring around the collar.

"We won't be late, Mom, promise."

"And make sure you change that shirt. In

case you win, everyone will be staring at you."

"Okay, Mom." Thomas could measure the degree of his mother's anxiety by how many instructions she gave. She was heading for a new record.

"Oh, and make sure McGrowl gets a nice long walk. We don't want him messing up the house."

"Will do," Thomas replied. As if McGrowl would ever go to the bathroom anywhere but exactly where he was supposed to. McGrowl knew how to use the toilet in Thomas's bathroom and even knew how to flush. He tended to view his walks as more entertainment and less business.

By the time she leaned over to give Thomas a hug for good luck, the boy and the dog were already halfway to Violet's. Thomas carried a small bag packed with a few essential sleuthing items: a flashlight, a flare for emergencies, and a small tool kit. The great Holmes always went into the field well prepared, and Thomas didn't intend to be any different. Tonight they would catch Muchnick and Von Vleck red-handed. Thomas felt sure of it.

It was a cold and windy night. No moon at all and hardly any stars. In the distance a lonely owl hooted softly. There wasn't a car on the road. All of a sudden, a twig snapped, and Thomas and McGrowl froze. The hair on the back of Thomas's neck stood straight up.

"Hands up, and don't say a word." The voice was low and quiet and sounded familiar. Violet couldn't contain herself any longer and started giggling. She had snuck up behind the two of them and had given at least one of them a terrible fright. McGrowl, of course, had immediately sensed it was Violet but decided not to spoil the girl's little joke. Boy and dog turned on the girl and started tickling her.

"Say uncle," Thomas said, but Violet was laughing too hard to say anything. At last she caught her breath. "Okay, I'm sorry. Really I am."

Suddenly, McGrowl caught the scent of something compelling and was off like a shot. The children had to run to catch up with him.

"What is it, boy?" And then Thomas looked down and noticed a small handkerchief. He had seen Muchnick carrying a similar handkerchief. McGrowl didn't have to sniff twice. Suspicion confirmed. They were onto something.

In their excitement both the children and their dog had failed to notice they were walking right into a trap. Muchnick was well aware that his little friends and their beloved dog were hot on his trail. He was leading them on a wild-goose chase.

"Look what I found," Violet called out excitedly. She had discovered, conveniently peek-

ing out from behind a fallen log, the rhine-
stone pin that Lily Von Vleck had used to hold
her angora sweater together. Another piece of
Muchnick's evil puzzle was falling into place.

McGrowl followed the scent right to the
edge of town. The dog pointed his big brown
proboscis at the old Compton mansion.
Proud and exhilarated, the dog waited for the
children to catch up to him. He had no idea he
was leading his favorite humans down a terrible blind alley, one from which they might
never return.

A pair of distant, unseen eyes watched
every move the children and the dog were
making. Never moving, never blinking, waiting patiently and calmly for the terrible thing
that was about to happen, the eyes stared at
the unsuspecting trio of friends.

CHAPTER TWELVE
Proceed with Caution

The imposing Victorian mansion occupied the top of the highest hill in Cedar Springs and stared down at the town like an angry giant. The house had been abandoned years ago after Lionel Compton died suddenly and none of his relatives could afford to pay the enormous taxes on it.

Everyone said the place was haunted. It certainly looked like it was. It had winding turrets, crumbling porches, and tattered curtains that billowed in and out of rows of broken windows. A lone streetlight cast an eerie shadow across the length of the house. Ghosts were a definite possibility. McGrowl wagged his tail furiously. The distinctive scent of the evil duo was everywhere.

"He says he thinks they're in there," Thomas interpreted.

"That's nice," Violet said tensely. "I wouldn't go in if you paid me forty trillion dollars."

"Let's just sneak around by the side and see what they're up to," Thomas gamely suggested.

"Let's not and say we did," Violet replied under her breath.

But Thomas crept over to a side porch and attempted to look through a small stained glass window. "I can't see anything from this angle," Thomas complained.

And then the boy started up the steps to the main entrance. McGrowl grabbed firmly on to his pants with his teeth.

"Good boy," Violet said quietly.

"Let go, McGrowl," Thomas protested, and attempted to wriggle free of the dog, which was, of course, impossible. "I'm only going up the steps. I'm not going inside. I just want to get a better look." The dog didn't budge.

The boy continued. "We'll all go together. We'll peek in for a second and then we'll leave. I promise. What could happen?"

McGrowl thought and thought and then, at last, gave in. The three explorers slowly climbed the rickety steps to the wide expanse of porch that ran along the entire front of the house.

McGrowl, Thomas, and Violet made their way carefully across the wide porch. Rotting boards beneath their feet creaked and groaned. Several of the boards were missing altogether.

Meanwhile, Muchnick and Von Vleck watched from their hideout down the street and around the corner. Muchnick could see precisely what they were doing. He twisted the dials on his high-powered binoculars, and the scene came into even sharper focus. "Goody, goody," he intoned dryly. The children were getting closer to the trap that had been so carefully set for them.

"Let me see," Miss Von Vleck begged impatiently and tried to grab the glasses away from Muchnick. The mayoral candidate, who had behaved so lovingly toward his fiancée earlier, held on to them firmly and attempted to kick the woman away with his large, wide feet.

"Get away from me, you nasty thing," he snarled. Von Vleck picked up a rock and attempted to hurl it right at him. "You do that and I'm never speaking to you again as long as I live," Muchnick threatened.

"Vhat do I care?" Von Vleck retorted. The two, who had only been posing as lovebirds for the mayoral race, were acting like babies fighting over a favorite pacifier.

"Wait a minute, something's happening." Muchnick spoke with such intensity that Lily Von Vleck dropped the rock. He put the binoculars up to his eyes and stared intently.

"In case anybody ca — ca — cares, I don't like this." Violet's teeth were chattering. The temperature seemed to drop a good ten degrees as soon as they approached the massive front door. There was an aura about the crumbling edifice. The air was thicker, and a delicate mist clung to it like the veil on an ancient, toothless bride.

Thomas tiptoed closer to the door. He had noticed it was ajar and wanted to get a look inside. His curiosity was definitely getting the better of him. Violet looked at her watch. And then she looked at Thomas. "I'm going home. I hate it here."

"Just one more minute," Thomas pleaded. "Look, I think I see something." Thomas noticed a flickering candle that Muchnick had placed in the living room. It sent a faint glow of light shimmering around the room. In one corner a rusty suit of armor glittered faintly in the candlelight. "Come on, it's really neat."

McGrowl suddenly turned to listen to a sound he could hear more clearly now. The evil duo, certain the dog was aware of their presence, stopped breathing altogether and waited for McGrowl to turn away.

Violet, overcome with curiosity herself, tiptoed several inches farther and joined Thomas at the threshold of the massive door. The combined weight of the two children was more than the floorboards could bear, which was exactly what Muchnick had counted on.

A terrible groaning sound was the only warning they received before Thomas and Violet crashed through the floor and down an endless, winding, darkened tunnel. Violet would have screamed if she could have caught her breath. Down they tumbled, farther and farther, into the black abyss.

Just when they thought they could go no farther, they landed with a resounding crash on a pile of something gooey, wet, and cold.

As McGrowl prepared to leap in after them, an iron grating closed quickly and firmly over the hole in the floor.

A terrible humming sound filled the air. It was, Thomas realized, the sound of an electromagnet. In the presence of the device the dog was reduced to an ordinary golden retriever. Prolonged contact with the device was potentially lethal for McGrowl. Thomas knew it. And so did Muchnick. The device had been cunningly rigged by Muchnick and his accomplice earlier in the day. The magnet was connected to a series of wires that twisted and wound their way through the tunnel, ending up at the grating itself. The main transmitter was hidden safely away, deep in the bowels of wherever they had fallen.

Everything was proceeding according to Muchnick's fiendish plan. The electromagnetic rays would prevent the dog from removing the grating and rescuing his friends.

From his hiding place safely down the road, Muchnick turned a switch. The sound from the electromagnet grew louder, and its current increased. Thomas and Violet held their hands to their ears to block out the terrible noise.

McGrowl felt himself growing weak. He had to get out of the area immediately. He could hear Muchnick laughing now, a terrible hollow laugh. Another voice joined in the merriment. "Congratulations, Mel, dollink, vee gonna be da mayor now." McGrowl headed straight for home. He had to tell Mr. and Mrs. Wiggins about the terrible danger their son and his friend were in.

McGrowl picked up speed. His powers were returning. An old woman lay injured and writhing in the middle of the road near an overturned wheelchair. He was moving so quickly he almost flew by her without stopping. She called out, "Help me, help me," in a small, sad voice. McGrowl screeched to a halt and ran over to see if he could help.

"Gotcha," the man said. McGrowl looked up and saw Muchnick standing right behind him. In his haste to come to the woman's rescue he had failed to notice the shadowy figure lurking behind a nearby tree. Another trap. In a flash the dog turned back to look at the old woman, who was already on her feet and fumbling with her purse. The elderly victim was none other then Lily Von Vleck in disguise.

The dog didn't stop to think. He pushed past Muchnick and started racing for the Wiggins's kitchen door. The evil stranger, caught off guard, wobbled and teetered and nearly lost his balance.

"Don't make a move or you're dead," Von Vleck growled through clenched teeth. The dog stopped in his tracks, turned to look at her, and held up his paws, pretending to obey. The woman threw off her bloody disguise and started deliberately and carefully toward McGrowl, holding a portable electromagnet in front of her. "Reach fer da sky, buster." Von Vleck had been watching too many Westerns on television. "Ve got ya dis time."

McGrowl held up his front paws, his thoughts racing. He had to buy some time. But how? He quickly calculated the distance from where he was standing to the safety of the Wiggins's house. Less than three hundred yards. So far, so good.

"No funny business, understand?" Von Vleck was upon him and nudging him with the end of her electromagnet. His brain cells were churning. At a speed of two hundred feet per second, with the wind favoring the direction of his retreat, he could make it home in less than — five seconds. He held his paws up higher and let loose a tremendous amount of doggy wind. The force of the expulsion nearly knocked Muchnick to the ground. It was McGrowl's secret weapon, and he had been saving it up since breakfast. Von Vleck grew dizzy from the smell and reached up to hold her nose. McGrowl had his five seconds.

He turned and raced for the door, zigzagging frantically left and right in the event Von Vleck recovered and was able to use her ray gun. She did. Holding her breath now, she raised the magnetic device quickly, squinted, and let forth with a massive blast of powerful rays. Just as McGrowl was about to hurl himself through the doggy door and into the safety of the Wiggins's kitchen, he was hit squarely behind the ears with a burst of dangerous negative ions.

The last thing he saw as he crumpled to the ground was Mrs. Wiggins leaving the front door and heading toward the garage. She was hurrying. She had to pick up Mr. Wiggins and get to the dog show. McGrowl tried to bark but couldn't even whimper. His legs were weak, and he was beginning to lose consciousness. Thomas's mother was trying not to jostle the victory cupcakes she was carrying. She never even looked up as she got into the car. If she had, she would have noticed the large yellow dog crumpling to the ground.

Von Vleck and Muchnick hid behind a mulberry bush and watched excitedly as Mrs. Wiggins drove off. They chortled wickedly. Together they tiptoed over and stared warily down at the defenseless animal. Von Vleck poked at McGrowl's flank with the tip of one of her pointy Manolo Blahnik shoes. He didn't stir. McGrowl was out cold. He was theirs.

Meanwhile, the passageway grew narrower, and Thomas and Violet were struggling to keep moving. "I don't want to upset you, but I think some snakes just tried to crawl up my leg," Thomas mentioned casually. Violet didn't mind snakes in general but didn't relish the thought of a bunch of them slithering around in the dark.

"Don't you have a flashlight in your emergency kit?" Violet inquired, panic rising in her voice. She could hear the slimy reptiles squishing this way and that as they wriggled effortlessly about in the mud that was everywhere. Thomas fumbled with the tool kit and the flare. He knew the light was in there somewhere. "Hurry, please," Violet said through clenched teeth.

"Found it," Thomas said, and finally pulled it out and flicked it on. Violet breathed a sigh of relief. Several large snakes, frightened by the light, slinked away into the recesses of the jagged walls.

Thomas examined the cavernous space into which they had fallen. Its walls were dark and craggy and filled with moss and lichen. The children immediately realized they were in some sort of underground cave. The air was dank and moist. The sound from the electromagnet echoed relentlessly from one rocky surface to the next.

They had landed in the middle of a series of enormous tunnels that ran under much of Cedar Springs. Thousands of years ago an underground river ran beneath the entire village. It carved out the endless network of grottoes and deeply etched canyons in which they were currently trapped.

Both Thomas and Violet quickly determined

that aside from a couple of scrapes and bruises, they suffered no broken bones. The damage was minimal. Thomas was already concocting a story to tell his mother to explain the presence of the muddy brown goop that was caked over every inch of their bodies.

They moved cautiously down a narrower section of the tunnel, and Thomas stumbled upon a trove of arrowheads, next to some ancient cooking pots. Tribes of Native Americans had once used the winding tunnels as a clever means of escape when bands of marauding invaders arrived from the north.

Eventually everybody forgot about the tunnels, which became the subject of a popular local folk tune called "Winding Tunnel Carry Me to Glory."

The children of Cedar Springs were required to learn the song in kindergarten but nobody really thought the tunnels actually existed. When Mel Muchnick was a child, he had come upon the tunnels himself and used them as a base of operations for his earliest evildoings.

As they made their way farther along the pathway that led to the electromagnet, Violet reminded Thomas that they had better turn off the flashlight and conserve batteries. "We could be in here for days, and that beam's looking pretty tired." Thomas agreed. Every night he had used the flashlight to send Violet messages in Morse code through their open bedroom windows. He wished he had remembered to put in a fresh supply of triple A batteries when he left the house.

They had to find the electromagnet and disable it. Only then could they notify McGrowl of their whereabouts — and only then could McGrowl come to their rescue. Without his help, there was no way they would ever be able to find their way out of the maze in which they were trapped.

The hum from the electromagnet was growing louder. They appeared to be heading in the right direction. Thomas switched off the light, plunging the two children once again into inky blackness. They inched forward.

Thomas bumped into what he thought at first was a boulder but upon closer investigation turned out to be a door carved into one of the walls of the grotto. The two of them pushed open the heavy door and proceeded cautiously.

Thomas turned on the flashlight for a few precious seconds and discovered a gas lamp hanging from the rather low ceiling. Violet located a match. She lit the lamp, and soon the area was bathed in a soft yellow glow.

They were in a room. A child-sized bed and nightstand were tucked into a corner. Colorful posters lined the walls and covered every surface of the little hideaway. A closer look revealed that the posters depicted a wide assortment of outlaws: Jesse James, Jack the Ripper, and Al Capone to name a few. *How strange*, Thomas thought. *What kind of child would have a room like this? And why?*

Violet picked up a little diary. It was so old its lock crumbled when she touched it. She opened it and turned a couple of yellowed pages. "Today I threw eggs at my cousin. . . . I refused to take a bath again. . . ." Thomas hurried over to look. "I frightened a little baby. . . ." He read further. "When I grow up I hereby promise to devote myself to being evil and making everybody miserable." This was no ordinary child. Thomas was getting a pretty good idea to whom the room belonged.

"It's creepy in here. Let's go," Violet urged. As they turned to leave he noticed a collection of random objects, piled helter-skelter along the wall nearest the door.

Thomas immediately spotted the collection of *Lost in Space* plates his mom's second cousin, Tweedy, had been missing for several days. Thomas also noticed the cigar box that held the class treasury. He looked inside. Not a penny of the money remained.

And then Thomas came upon the little ceramic jar he had made his mother in second grade. The jar was supposed to hold pencils, but Mrs. Wiggins kept it in a drawer in the kitchen and used it to keep the money she gave to delivery boys and the occasional UNICEF trick-or-treater.

"Of course," Thomas said as much to himself as to Violet. "Muchnick has been using this as a storage room for all the stuff he's been stealing from everybody. This must have been his hideout when he was little."

"You're probably right," Violet concurred.

"Now whadaya say we try to locate the electromagnet and tell McGrowl where we are. I don't know about you, but I wouldn't mind getting out of this place alive."

As the two children hurried out of the room they couldn't help but notice a framed diploma hanging on the wall. It read: "The school system of Cedar Springs proudly congratulates Milton Smudge upon his completion . . ."

Thomas reached into his pocket and pulled out the little scrap of paper he had discovered in Mabel Rabkin's office. The mysterious letters "lton S" suddenly leaped out at him. Of course! Thomas's mind was racing. They were the middle five letters of the name on the diploma. Milton Smudge, the unhappiest boy in school. "Muchnick broke into Rabkin's office to steal his own folder!" Thomas exclaimed. Everything was falling into place.

"But why would anybody want to steal his own records?" Violet asked.

"Maybe this is why," Thomas said as he picked up a faded, yellowing newspaper article from a pile of clippings neatly arranged on a nearby table. The article was all about little Miltie Smudge, as he was called, and all the terrible things he had done when he was a little boy.

No wonder Muchnick changed his name and attempted to destroy all traces of his nasty childhood. Who would ever have voted for him? And then Thomas recalled an expression his father often used, "The child is father to the man." Thomas had to admit that in this case the expression seemed especially apt.

He pocketed the diploma along with enough evidence of the man's thievery to put Muchnick and Von Vleck safely behind bars for a good long time. And then he and Violet struggled to close the door that held the secrets of Muchnick's awful childhood.

CHAPTER THIRTEEN
Almost Famous

Mr. and Mrs. Wiggins had, of course, been the very first people to arrive at the Big Dog Show. The bleachers that lined the far end of the soccer field where the event would take place were completely empty. They arranged their numerous possessions carefully. The picnic hamper went under the seats, the blanket went over their laps, and the padded, battery-powered cushions they brought went under their keesters.

Henry Wiggins smiled contentedly. He put

his feet up and reflected. The response to his commercial was enormous. Mr. Lundquist had made him the head of the entire media division. He had a raise, a big promotion, a wonderful wife, and a son who was about to win first prize in a dog show. *Things*, he said to himself, *couldn't possibly be going better*.

Meanwhile, Thomas and Violet wandered farther down the twisting path of the dried-up riverbed. By now they were getting used to the dreadful humming noise. What they couldn't get used to was the sense that they were getting themselves deeper into a situation that held no favorable outcome.

The air in the tunnel was thick with moisture and dust. Breathing was already becoming difficult.

Thomas's legs were weak, and he had a pounding headache. Violet was so exhausted she almost fell asleep standing up. But still they continued.

In a darkened room, in a tidy little house that looked like every other house on the tidy little block, McGrowl opened his eyes. He was sore and tried to stretch his gangly limbs. He immediately realized he was bound from head to toe with a heavy rope. He struggled, unsuccessfully, to remove it.

"Isn't dat cute?" Von Vleck whispered. "He tinks he can escape. Ho-ho." Muchnick rubbed his icy hands together and smiled menacingly. By the time the bedraggled children discovered a way out, if indeed they ever did, he would be mayor. The town would be in his clutches, and with the help of the dog, nothing and no one would be able to stop him in his quest to take over Cedar Springs — and eventually the world.

Things, he said to himself, *couldn't possibly be going better.*

And if the children never escaped? This thought had definitely occurred to Muchnick. He had to admit the prospect didn't exactly fill him with dread. Quite the opposite. In fact, his eyes twinkled as he thought how good he would look in the gray pin-striped suit he would wear to commemorate the brief but tragic lives of the plucky little boy and girl. He would commission a statue the instant he was elected mayor.

"No funny bizness, poochie," Von Vleck crisply announced. The portable electromagnet was poised on a nearby windowsill and ready for use on a moment's notice. McGrowl knew the desperate woman wouldn't hesitate to use it again.

And then McGrowl heard the snapping of a twig and the familiar sound of a cat's paw landing on what sounded like a window ledge. One sniff confirmed his suspicion. He stole a furtive glance in the direction of the window. Sitting on the ledge, right next to the portable electromagnet, was none other than the dreaded neighborhood cat. She had smelled McGrowl and had wandered over to torment him. The dog had never been so glad to see anyone in his entire life.

Fortunately, Von Vleck was utterly unaware of the presence of the cat. She was too busy staring at McGrowl and making sure he didn't move a muscle.

Thomas and Violet moved cautiously down a narrow passageway. Their flashlight was so dim now they could barely see, but it was bright enough to frighten a nest of sleeping bats. The winged creatures awakened suddenly and madly darted about in all directions. Violet and Thomas tried to duck.

They knew the bats were harmless, but the feeling of frantic leathery wings beating against their faces was something neither of them would forget for a long, long time. The bats careened farther down the tunnel. The children moved forward until they came upon a small opening. A giant boulder blocked all but a small corner. Thomas peered inside and held his light up. The giant electromagnet machine stared out at them from its hiding place. It roared and hummed and sent forth a shower of sparks as it labored to generate its powerful force field.

Thomas and Violet pushed and pulled with all their might, but they couldn't seem to budge the enormous rock that blocked their entry. Thomas tried to wedge himself between the rock and the wall. He twisted and strained. "Just a few more inches," he grunted.

Violet was pulling and pushing, too, but the rock wasn't moving. And then Thomas's flashlight failed altogether, and again they were plunged into darkness. A faint red glow from the machine shone on Thomas's grimy face. He pulled and pushed with one final effort, and suddenly, the rock shifted. Violet had to leap back to avoid being crushed, but at last there was room for the two children to squeeze through the tiny opening.

They ran to the electromagnet and immediately began to remove its outer shell. They had to penetrate the inner workings of the powerful device and shut off the generator whining and whirring deep within its core. In the murky darkness of the cavern it was impossible for Thomas to see what he was doing.

"The flare," Violet remembered suddenly. "Didn't you pack a flare?" Thomas raced to pull out the small emergency candle he had tucked away in his bag. Thomas guessed it would hold out for two or three minutes. He hoped he was right. If his calculations were correct it would take just about that long to finish his crucial task. Or so he hoped.

The flare's bluish light flickered against the walls of the cavern. Violet stood next to the boy, handing him tools as he called for them.

"Pliers."

"How's it going?" Violet asked, trying not to panic.

"Don't ask," Thomas answered curtly.

"I hate to be a pest, but I'm having a little trouble breathing," Violet said.

"Screwdriver," Thomas said as he removed a large piece of the outer casing and prepared to begin the delicate job of disengaging the inner core. "Yeah, I'm having trouble breathing myself."

"What do you think we should do?" Violet said as she carefully helped Thomas lift away a section of molded steel that had been riveted to the bottom of the device. It was the last barrier standing between Thomas and success.

"I dunno. Breathe less?" answered Thomas. It was cold and clammy in the tunnel, but beads of sweat poured from Thomas's forehead. All of a sudden, a tiny switch came into view. The boy reached out with a trembling finger and turned it off.

The relentless droning sound of the magnet came to an immediate halt, and the cavern was plunged into silence. The sounds of bat wings flapping and snakes slithering about were a welcome change. Violet noticed that her own breathing had become labored.

She opened her mouth to speak, but Thomas shushed her. He was sending McGrowl a message. And for the first time since they had fallen into that dreaded tunnel, McGrowl was receiving it. The message let McGrowl know precisely where the children were, that they were safe, and that they didn't have much time left.

Von Vleck stared at McGrowl. McGrowl stared at the cat. He made a quick but calculated decision. He started barking loudly. Then he leaped to his feet and, in a single thrust of his powerful limbs, tore through the strong ropes that bound him. As Muchnick heard the noise and came running into the room, Von Vleck reached frantically for the switch to turn on the portable electromagnet. The cat, startled by the dog, made a leap away from the window, knocking into the device. As Von Vleck reached for the switch, the electromagnet teetered and fell out the window. Before either of the evil duo had a chance to retrieve it, McGrowl was out the window like a bolt of lightning, hurtling toward the mansion.

"We're getting the dog now. I'm killing you later," Muchnick screamed as he and his accomplice sped out the back of the house. They had to get to McGrowl before he got to the children.

They ran to a nearby grating that covered what appeared to be an entrance to a sewer. The entrance led to a secret passageway to the series of underground tunnels in which Thomas and Violet were trapped. "Faster, faster," Muchnick grunted through clenched teeth.

In seconds the evil duo had lowered themselves down a ladder to a waiting motorcycle. Soon they were careening forward through the tunnels in a desperate attempt to head off McGrowl before he had a chance to save the children.

McGrowl arrived at the mansion and instantly started ripping apart the bars that covered the opening through which the children had fallen. A beeper sounded in Muchnick's pocket. Ever the master of devious planning, Muchnick had rigged the device to go off the moment the bars were disturbed.

"Faster, stupid," Von Vleck screamed into Muchnick's ear as they sped through the cavernous tunnels.

"Sticks and stones, sticks and stones," he yelled in reply. And then he shoved the woman with such force he nearly knocked her over. Von Vleck desperately grabbed Muchnick's head, nearly blocking his already dim view of the path ahead. The speedometer on the motorcycle read eighty miles per hour as the evil strangers sped forward over the bumpy terrain.

McGrowl hurtled through the darkened tunnels with the speed of a roaring locomotive. Already his superhearing could detect the distant sounds of the children's labored breathing. He didn't have a minute to lose. His sensitive eyes were able to capture and magnify the few available microns of light trapped within the cavern. He quickly spotted the children's footprints and raced to save them.

Thomas and Violet heard the approaching *whoosh* as McGrowl drew nearer. "What if he doesn't see us?" Violet gasped. The supply of air in the underground chamber was almost gone, and even Thomas was becoming light-headed.

And then Muchnick's motorcycle turned a sharp corner. Von Vleck spotted the tornado-like vortex that was McGrowl speeding directly at them. Just as the motorcycle and the dog were about to collide, Von Vleck reached into her pocketbook and pulled out yet another portable electromagnet. Before you could blink, she had that device up and running and aimed right at her nemesis. "Gotcha," she cried triumphantly.

In an instant the tornado that had been

McGrowl turned into a tired and somewhat shaky golden retriever. The dog didn't need to hear the buzzing to understand immediately what had transpired. He had once again been successfully zapped by the electromagnetic force.

Thomas and Violet used their last remaining breath to call out for help. Even without his superhearing McGrowl could hear their tired cries. He tried to head in the direction of their voices. Although hidden behind a solid wall of granite, they were no more than thirty feet from where he stood.

"Vere do you tink you're going, blondie?" Von Vleck taunted as she turned up the intensity on her transmitter. McGrowl felt as though he weighed a thousand pounds. Every muscle in his body ached with exhaustion, but he continued to drag his tired frame toward his cherished friends. He could tell from their voices that he didn't have much time left.

McGrowl was beginning to lose hope. In another few seconds he would pass out from the effects of the electromagnet. Thomas' and Violet's chances of survival were looking dimmer and dimmer. Von Vleck walked slowly toward him, aiming the magnet right at him. The rays were so powerful the poor dog could barely stand upright.

Muchnick was besotted with excitement. He had won. Or so he thought.

Suddenly, a low rumbling sound filled the cavern. The vibrations generated by the electromagnet had weakened the already crumbling ceiling right above Muchnick's and Von Vleck's heads. Dust and pebbles began to trickle down. Muchnick and Von Vleck ignored the menacing sound.

"Soon you'll be mine," he gloated. "And those horrible children will cease to exist. Oh, happy day." Muchnick grabbed Von Vleck, and the two of them began to dance wildly about, screaming and yelling and laughing. They were blissfully unaware of the disaster their hysterical gyrations were about to wreak upon them.

Suddenly, rocks started raining down from above. Big ones. Little ones. Sharp ones and smooth ones. The walls were caving in! Dust was everywhere.

Neither Muchnick nor Von Vleck were anywhere to be seen, apparently buried under a mountain of rubble. The portable electromagnet lay smashed and ruined under a pile of rocks.

McGrowl felt his superpowers surging back into his tired limbs. He hadn't a moment to waste. He tunneled through the pile of debris that surrounded him.

In less than a second he burrowed a tunnel right through to his friends. There they were, Thomas and Violet, crumpled on the floor in a sad little heap. But they were alive. The boy managed to lift his head and whisper hoarsely to his favorite companion, "I knew you'd save us, McGrowl. I never doubted you for a second."

In the twinkling of an eye McGrowl had Thomas and Violet on his sturdy shoulders. Soon the three friends were flying through the tunnels, back to the tiny entrance, and as far away from the front porch as McGrowl could manage.

The constant drone of the sonic waves had weakened not just the ceiling above Muchnick and Von Vleck but the ancient walls that supported the maze of tunnels and caverns in which the children had been trapped as well. As the walls and ceilings collapsed, torrents of raging water, previously held at bay by the tunnels, were suddenly released.

The very place where Thomas and Violet had stood only moments ago was transformed instantly into a churning mass of earth and stone. The decrepit old house began to crumble. The ground beneath the fleeing trio began to tremble.

They were half a mile away from the mansion when it happened. What sounded like a dozen rapid claps of thunder caused McGrowl to slow down and the children to cover their ears. Weakened by the roiling destruction beneath it, the old house was falling in upon itself. Within seconds, the Compton mansion, Muchnick's childhood sanctuary, was reduced to a dusty pile of bricks and wood. Given the cataclysmic nature of the event, it seemed likely that Muchnick and Von Vleck had suffered a similar fate.

The dog stopped for a moment, and the three friends took a long look back. Thomas and Violet watched in awed silence. Even McGrowl had to admit the call had been closer than he could possibly have imagined. And then he sent Thomas a message.

"Translation, please," Violet said, feeling

somewhat left out. Thomas quickly explained that McGrowl wanted to know if they could still go to the dog show. It was starting in five minutes. Negative ions and a near brush with death weren't about to slow this puppy down. The dog sent Thomas an image of the largest silver trophy he had ever seen. Thomas beamed.

"I wouldn't miss it for anything" was Thomas's instant reply. McGrowl let out an excited woof and took off like a speeding bullet as Violet and Thomas held on for dear life.

In another second they were careening past Thomas's house. The dog reminded the children to hold on even tighter and started making a series of bounding leaps over streets, people, traffic jams, and even buildings. They had to duck to avoid a gaggle of geese that was heading south for the winter. In another second the soccer field came into view. Thomas could see the crowded bleachers and hear Principal Grimble's resounding bull-horn.

They landed just behind the viewing stands and scrambled madly to get to their places.

Thomas's mother spotted them immediately. She smiled, pointed at her watch, and shook her head. They had arrived with just five seconds to spare.

CHAPTER FOURTEEN
The Greatest Show on Earth

The entire Wiggins family looked on proudly while McGrowl and Thomas stood at attention. Principal Grimble bellowed over the PA system. "And now, a really big hand for our talented finalistsssss."

Thomas sent McGrowl a message that let him know how proud he was of him for getting this far and that it didn't really matter whether they won. McGrowl's reply was brief. He told Thomas that defeat was unthinkable, and that was simply all there was to it. The boy grinned from ear to ear.

Only McGrowl, Rumpelstiltskin the Chihuahua, and Lewis Musser's dog, Spike, remained. The crowd grew still.

McGrowl and Thomas watched closely as the Chihuahua and his owner, Esther Mueller, executed a series of complicated maneuvers. Esther ran to one end of the platform while Rumpelstiltskin sat obediently at the other. And then, on a cue from Esther's mother, Louise, "Lady of Spain" started blaring over the loudspeakers.

Esther whipped out a large red handkerchief from her pocket and started twirling it about like a matador. She stomped her feet, shuffled around, and shouted "*Olé*."

The Chihuahua ran toward the little girl and attempted to butt his tiny head into the kerchief while Esther swirled and dodged. The judges nodded their heads in approval. The idea of a bullfight between a little girl and a dog the size of a flea certainly was original.

The crowd cheered eagerly but was somewhat disappointed when Rumpelstiltskin lay down in the middle of the song and refused to pretend to be a bull one second longer. At last Principal Grimble came to the rescue. "Congratulations are in order, folks. That is the smartest insect I have ever seen performing in a dog show." The crowd broke into peals of nervous laughter. "Wait a minute — was that a dog? Coulda fooled me." The crowd applauded politely as Esther carried Rumpelstiltskin off the field. Lewis Musser and Spike trotted into view.

Spike and Lewis ran once around the platform in perfect step. Even McGrowl was impressed. When Lewis hopped, Spike hopped. When Lewis marched double time, Spike followed suit. It certainly was an auspicious beginning. *What*, Thomas wondered, *would they do next?*

And then Lewis pulled out an oversized Frisbee and engaged Spike in a lively round of toss and catch.

Lewis looked about as smug as the cat that swallowed the canary when the crowd cheered and Principal Grimble made his announcement: "Well, folksss, we have a front-runner, and his name is Spike." At this point Lewis picked up Spike and started dancing around with him and shouting "Yes!" The crowd chanted "Spike, Spike, Spike," and Lewis's family threw handfuls of confetti all over the place.

Mr. and Mrs. Wiggins looked anxiously at each other. Neither wanted to admit what they were secretly thinking: Not even McGrowl would be capable of beating a performance like the one they had just witnessed. Poor Thomas would be so disappointed.

The moment of truth was at hand. Lewis and Spike left the field. Lewis's mom was already trying to get his hair to lay down so that he would look good when he had his picture taken in the winner's circle.

Thomas gave McGrowl an affectionate pat. Determination shone in the dog's eager eyes. This time he would do his boy proud. Every muscle in his awesome body was ready to spring into action.

McGrowl and Thomas warmed up with a few cursory but meticulously executed maneuvers. Thomas lay on his back and thrust McGrowl into the air with his feet. As the dog flew through the air, he turned a perfect somersault and landed smartly on his hind legs. Then Thomas stood on his head, and McGrowl executed a flawless swan dive through the boy's outstretched legs.

Both boy and dog stood up and took a bow in perfect unison. McGrowl and Thomas turned left and then right with absolutely mirror-perfect symmetry. They basked in the cheering of the happy throng. The hours of planning and rehearsing had paid off. McGrowl was giving the performance of a lifetime.

Lewis Musser looked on in horror and disbelief as Thomas took out his Frisbee and threw it into the air as hard as he could. McGrowl easily caught it between his teeth. Instead of carrying it back to Thomas and dropping it at his feet like any normal dog, McGrowl ran around in a quick series of circling movements and let go of the shiny red platter at just the right second. It went flying into the stands with enough spin on it to come boomeranging back at McGrowl in a graceful arcing motion. The dog was throwing and catching his own Frisbee. Lewis was apoplectic with rage.

"Will you look at that!" Principal Grimble

hollered into his bullhorn. He was so excited he forgot to overenunciate. "Never in all my years as host of this wonderful event do I re- member such a talented performance by a canine."

"What a dog!" Mr. Wiggins exclaimed. He was so happy he grabbed Mrs. Wiggins and hugged her until she thought she would burst. Roger decided, then and there, that he would ask Thomas to let McGrowl be the basketball team's new mascot.

How, Lewis wondered, could that stupid lit- tle Thomas Wiggins beat him at anything? No, this couldn't be happening. It was too hu- miliating. Suddenly, he sprang into action. He reached under his seat and pulled out a little yellow bundle. Carefully, he held it on his lap and removed a small fuzzy blanket, revealing none other than the neighborhood cat.

Lewis was taking no chances. He had re- membered the disastrous effect the cat had on McGrowl at the trials and had brought along the irritating feline as an insurance policy. She had just returned home from her terrifying encounter with McGrowl when Lewis catnapped her and brought her to the event. The cat stretched, yawned, and began to purr softly.

McGrowl had just started a dizzying combination of acrobatic moves when his superhearing detected the familiar purring of the dreaded neighborhood cat. But the desensitizing exercises had worked, and McGrowl's heart didn't skip a single beat. His mind remained clear and calm.

McGrowl was right in the middle of a back flip when he let Thomas know that the sight of the neighborhood cat was no longer a big deal for him. He continued twirling around madly. Thomas sent back a short message: *Congratulations!*

Lewis couldn't believe his eyes. The cat

was having no effect whatsoever on the dog. It was time for plan B. The angry boy held up a little plastic whistle he had been hiding in his pocket and blew a quick series of short notes. No one even noticed.

Except, of course, the entire front row of the bleachers. Thomas hadn't thought twice about it, but everyone occupying the front section of seats had two things in common: One, they were all friends of Lewis. And two, they all appeared to be extremely fat. That is, their coats all seemed to be having a hard time covering their bulging bellies. Lewis blew the whistle again, and every person in the front row suddenly removed their coats and revealed Lewis's big surprise.

Sitting on the laps of all forty-six people occupying the entire front row of the bleachers were forty-six cats. McGrowl glanced over, absolutely confident that nothing in the world could possibly stop him now. He had planned.

He had rehearsed. He was prepared for anything. Anything but the dizzying array of aggravating tabbies and Siameses and strays that stared back at him, yowling and hissing to beat the band.

The dog commanded every muscle in his body to continue, but his legs were beginning to shake, and his ears were twitching. Thomas recognized the telltale signs. Forty-six cats waving their tails, grooming their fur, and purring insolently was more than one dog could stand. Certainly more than McGrowl could stand. Thomas understood. He really did.

Lewis smiled, Spike wagged his stubby little tail, and Mr. and Mrs. Musser winked at each other. They didn't care how Lewis did it. They wanted that trophy, and they wanted it bad. They had all the money in the world. But they didn't have a dog show trophy on the mantel.

"Something is happening," Principal Grimble announced tersely. He could barely catch his breath. No one in the crowd dared move a muscle. All eyes were focused on the little boy and his amazing dog, who stood as still as a statue, staring at the cats as if his life depended on it. "Ladies and gentlemen, this is turning out to be the dog show of the decade. No, the century."

Thomas held his breath. He had heard the expression "time stood still" but had never actually experienced the phenomenon until this very moment.

McGrowl found himself in a massive state of utter confusion. *To win or not to win, that was the question. Whether to suffer the slings and arrows of outrageous fortune — go for the cats, lose the race, and hate himself in the morning.* He inched forward. Or — *win the race, lose the cats, and also hate himself in the morning.* He inched backward. *Didn't winning the race mean more to Thomas than anything? True, very true. Good dog. Forget the cats. Win the race. No, no. Go for the cats. Lose the race. Yes. Yes.*

McGrowl had such a headache he ceased thinking altogether and considered going to sleep. In another second it would all be over. *Second place isn't that bad,* Thomas thought. McGrowl heard and was too ashamed to reply. He couldn't bear disappointing Thomas yet again. He started running. The crowd held their collective breath. Was the dog winding up for an even more amazing feat? Or was he simply giving up and running away as fast as he could?

Mr. Wiggins no longer hugged Mrs. Wiggins. He wrapped his arms around himself and seemed to be moaning. Was McGrowl deserting the field?

McGrowl ran up and down the front row — faster than a speeding bullet. He growled and he grimaced and he threatened with lightning speed. He was back on the platform and ready to continue with his spectacular performance before anyone but Thomas had noticed what was happening. Forty-six terrified cats were speeding out of the stadium, and Lewis Musser was beginning to cry. He blew his nose loudly and pretended he had gotten dust in his eyes. McGrowl could see a tear streaming down his face and felt bad, but just for a second.

McGrowl finished his routine with a breathtaking series of rollovers and scissors kicks that made even Thomas gasp with delight. The roar of the crowd was deafening. Mr. Wiggins jumped into the air and nearly fell off the platform. Lewis Musser and Spike were so mortified they pulled their matching sweaters over their heads and tried to look invisible.

Thomas and McGrowl sailed through the rest of their routine with the skill and grace of a pair of championship figure skaters. No child and his companion had ever completed the challenge with such aplomb. At one point the dog executed a hairpin maneuver on the tip of one paw, the doggy equivalent of a "wheelie," and the crowd let out an ecstatic roar. McGrowl was in his groove.

McGrowl did a series of flips and cart-wheels while catching and returning the Fris-bee all by himself. Thomas stood by proudly, waving and bowing. Principal Grimble jumped up and down with such abandon he nearly twisted his knee. Miss Thompson forgot what she was doing and threw a batch of uncor-rected midterms up in the air.

And then it was over. The crowd was screaming, Principal Grimble's bullhorn was screeching, and confetti filled the air. Thomas and McGrowl looked at each other so calmly and peacefully they might as well have been at home alone in their room. Thomas let McGrowl know he was bursting with pride.

McGrowl let Thomas know he was happier at that moment than he had ever been in his life.

Thomas was so excited he barely noticed the trophy being handed to him. Suddenly, everyone was shaking his hand and congratulating him. Mr. Wiggins had to pull the car around and take every single thing out of the trunk to make room for the beloved shining silver award. McGrowl ran up and down and received more pats from more people than he believed possible.

The crowd had given the boy and the dog a standing ovation that lasted more than seven minutes and caused the principal to announce a school holiday for the following day. "Tomorrow will be declared McGrowl Day," he proudly asserted. "And we shall all spend it at home with our dogsss. And those of us who don't have dogsss" — he paused meaningfully — "will just have to get one. I suggest the shelter around the corner."

McGrowl was a hero, and Thomas was a winner. Mrs. Wiggins held her arms out and embraced Thomas and Violet and then McGrowl. She didn't even notice the fact that they were extremely dirty — at least for three or four seconds. "What happened to you?" she exclaimed loudly, and quickly brushed herself off.

Violet opened her mouth to speak. "You'll never believe —"

Thomas interrupted. "Well, we were working on our science project," he began. And then he proceeded to tell the part where they came upon some arrowheads. He decided to leave out the part about free-falling almost a hundred feet down a tunnel in order to find them. He left out a couple of other things, too. Like the snakes, and the lack of oxygen, and being trapped underground without any lights.

He also failed to mention the fiendish electromagnetic device and Muchnick's secret boyhood hideaway. If she knew even one-tenth of what they had been through, neither one of them would ever be able to leave the house for the rest of their lives.

Mrs. Wiggins was already sufficiently hysterical over the condition of their clothing. "Never," she said in her most serious tone of voice, "have I witnessed such an accumulation of stubborn stains and greasy buildup."

And then they were in the car and heading for home. Perfect strangers came out of their houses to cheer and wave. Thomas and McGrowl were invited to appear on *Simply Cedar,* the popular local talk show. Even Flinty McFlint's radio hour dedicated most of its program that night to "Thomas and his wonderful dog."

CHAPTER FIFTEEN
Pleasant Dreams

The evening news was abuzz with exciting developments as well. The Compton mansion was the lead story. It had collapsed, as Channel Six incorrectly reported, from an infestation of giant warrior termites.

Muchnick and Von Vleck seemed to have disappeared into thin air. Repeated calls to campaign headquarters weren't returned, and a missing persons report was filed with the police.

Stanley Fitch was declared the winner in the city's first undisputed mayoral race. He was quick to point out that the disappearance of Muchnick coincided strangely with an abrupt halt in the robberies that had plagued the little town.

Officer Nelson breathed a sigh of relief. He decided that with crime once more on the decline, he would stay on the force. No more supermarket managing for this man in blue. The news ended with a brief but exciting mention of the fact that Thomas Wiggins and his dog, McGrowl, had won the dog show hands down in the single most exciting performance that had ever been witnessed.

McGrowl and Thomas stared quietly at the gleaming silver trophy on the mantel. Yes, it had been hard work. But seeing the smile on his boy's face had made every minute of the exhausting day well worth the effort. Thomas hurried upstairs to brush and floss.

"Sleep tight, don't let the termites bite — I mean bedbugs." Mrs. Wiggins finished calling out their nightly ritual and went outside to wash and wax the car.

Thomas and McGrowl were resting peacefully in Thomas's bed. Thomas could barely keep his eyes open. He looked sleepily over at McGrowl. *Trophies were nice,* he thought, *but friends were nicer.* Especially furry yellow friends that slept on your bed and protected you. McGrowl snuggled deeper into the warm furrow between the boy's arm and his side.

Thomas thought about the dog show. Then he thought about his adventures under the mansion. And he thought about how glad he was that Muchnick and Von Vleck were no longer in the picture.

" 'Night, McGrowl," he whispered. The boy looked long and hard into the dog's big brown eyes. "What in the world would I ever do without you?"

McGrowl looked at Thomas gratefully and then rolled over onto his back and assumed the "scratch my stomach if you love me" position. The boy scratched, and as if such a thing were actually possible, the dog seemed to purr contentedly.

The air was crisp and cool, and the smell of autumn leaves burning in the distance tickled Thomas's nose. Life was very good, indeed. And then Thomas fell fast asleep.

A light rain began to fall. McGrowl thought he saw a couple of snowflakes mixed in with it. Soon there would be sledding and snowmen and evenings by the fireplace.

The dog was breathing deep, quiet breaths, and his eyelids closed. He, too, was weary from a long, hard day. He rested a watchful paw on Thomas's shoulder. Thomas's nightlight filled the room with a gentle glow. Dog and boy snored peacefully at last. Identical dreams filled their heads. A pile of mashed potatoes. Ice-skating. Christmas dinner. Rock climbing. An evil stranger climbing a hill and peering back down at them.

The dog awoke in a flash. In that moment he knew. The strangers were alive. The dog could sense them as clearly as if they were standing directly in front of him. They were bruised and they were battered, but they were very much alive. No avalanche was big enough to destroy them.

Thomas stirred fitfully. The boy, too, was aware that the forces of evil that threatened their very existence had subsided only momentarily.

The dog eased himself into the comforter, rested his head on Thomas's pillow, and closed his eyes again. It had been a long hard day, and he would need all his energy to fight the evil strangers when they next returned.

Rain turned to snow. Powdery white drifts formed in yards and streets. In the distance a train chugged lazily by. McGrowl was asleep. He dreamed of a day without evil. A day without fear. A day of peace.

That day would come. But not for a long, long time.

Bob Balaban is a respected producer, director, writer, and actor. He produced and costarred in Robert Altman's Oscar®-winning film *Gosford Park*, which was named Best British Film of 2001 at the British Academy Awards. He has appeared in *Close Encounters of the Third Kind*, *Absence of Malice*, *Deconstructing Harry*, *Waiting for Guffman, Ghost World*, and *The Majestic* among many other films and has appeared on *Seinfeld* several times as the head of NBC. Mr. Balaban produced and directed the feature films *Parents* and *The Last Good Time*, which won best film and best director awards at the Hamptons International Film Festival. Mr. Balaban lives in New York with his wife, writer Lynn Grossman, and his daughters, Hazel and Mariah. At the moment, he is canineless, but he is looking forward to a close encounter with his own actual dog, not just one of the literary kind.